DARKNESS
AWAKENED

A DARKNESS NOVEL

Katie Reus

Darkness Awakened/Katie Reus. -- 1st ed.
ISBN-13: 9781493600915
ISBN-10: 1493600915

For Kari Walker. Thank you for always being in my corner.

CHAPTER ONE

Finn Stavros didn't bother to wipe the blood from his blade before turning on another Akkadian demon emerging from the interior of the dark warehouse. Adrenaline punched through him, a hard and vicious surge as he faced off with this monster. He'd already killed two of the demons so that just left two more. He hadn't planned to shift to his animal form tonight but it looked like he had no choice. He would be more powerful as a wolf and this fight needed to end quickly. Before any nosy or unsuspecting humans stumbled on them.

After following one of these wretched things from his casino, Finn had expected a fast kill. Not to stumble on more of them in this abandoned warehouse.

Dropping his blade to the concrete floor, Finn tensed as his body underwent the change. Gray and white fur sprouted as his bones and ligaments broke, shifted and realigned. The shift was short and momentarily painful, but gave way to a heady rush of raw power that pulsed through him. Seconds later, he stood on all fours, his clothes and shoes shredded around him.

As a born Alpha and leader of his pack, he had a higher element of strength and speed than his brethren.

He might be only one hundred and fifty years old, but when he'd killed his treacherous uncle and taken control over his pack, Finn had absorbed his uncle's strength as well.

The floor was cold beneath his paws and a sensitized awareness flowed through him in steady waves. Every sense was enhanced. The horned, clawed demon creature stared at him hungrily, but Finn would be the only thing walking out of this building alive tonight. These freakish bastards might have the ability to glamorize themselves to humans—making themselves look not only normal, but beautiful—but as another supernatural being, Finn could see their true form clearly.

Some days he *really* wished he couldn't.

It was disturbing to see a human sidling up to these monsters completely unaware that they'd be the demon's dinner.

Baring his teeth, Finn snarled at the reptilian skinned being with gaunt cheeks, glowing yellow eyes, clawed hands and clawed feet. This one was only six feet tall but some of them grew to seven feet. Like the last two he'd just killed. And he could smell them a mile away. Their putrid, sulfuric stench was nauseating. The past month had brought out too many of these things for him and his pack to ignore. At one time they'd been the stuff of nightmares. Like the boogie man; scary but in an abstract way. Not anymore.

Locked away in hell millennia ago, they didn't belong on this plane of earth. After being caged for so long, it seemed as if they were consumed with a powerful bloodlust that robbed them of control once they started to feed or hunt. They were threatening the secret existence of all supernatural beings with their carelessness. Finn didn't know what had released them from hell, but he planned to find out and make sure they were sent back where they belonged.

With a snarl, the creature extended its claws and advanced. Tensing his muscles and using all the strength in his hind legs, Finn lunged forward, bracing for the pain. He could take being sliced up by this thing. The key to killing them was doing it quick. The key to *any* fight was ending it quick. For some reason these demons liked to fight one on one. So even though he scented another one in the warehouse, it wouldn't make a move until either Finn or the demon emerged from this battle victorious.

He flew through the air and ripped a chunk of its shoulder clean off. The creature howled eerily but swiped his claws down Finn's side. The slashing pain burned through him as his flesh ripped away. But the sting only enraged his inner wolf more.

Growling low in his throat, Finn turned in the air before he slammed onto the ground.

Strike fast and hard.

He pounced again. This time he managed to clamp his jaws down on the creature's throat. Biting down, he tasted flesh and blood. The thick fluid was foul, with more than a hint of sulfur in it.

He ripped through tendons and bone and jerked back, tearing off its head and killing it instantly. Before he could spin around, he felt the impact of the last remaining creature landing on his back. It sunk its claws deep into his ribcage.

Roaring, he twisted and tried to dislodge the thing, but its claws only pierced more deeply. Knives of pain splintered through his body, making his nerve endings scream, but he ignored it. He'd heal. This thing was going to die one way or another.

Rolling back, he used his weight to pin it to the ground underneath him. As it slammed against the concrete, the creature's claws retracted, giving Finn the chance to dodge away.

Jumping to his feet, he lunged before it had a chance to rise. His jaws opened and clamped on the creature's neck, severing its head in one clean stroke. Faster than he'd killed the first.

His heart raced as he swiveled in each direction, looking for more danger around the abandoned warehouse. Wooden crates were stacked in two separate corners. Above him a cobwebbed skeleton of steel stretched across the ceiling. Since these things couldn't climb or fly like some vampires, he wasn't worried about an aerial attack. Continuing to scan the darkness of the desolate building that was little more than a metal box, his inner wolf slowly calmed when he scented nothing else unusual. He was especially thankful he couldn't scent any humans. These days it seemed that all of them had phones with video or camera capabilities and the last thing any supernatural beings needed was someone to record what had just happened.

As he shifted back to his human form, a new smell filled the air. He paused, ready to fight again, until the familiar scent of Gabriel, his pack Guardian grew nearer. He must have just arrived because his Guardian wouldn't have let him fight alone. It went against Gabriel's nature and pack law.

Ignoring the already fading pain, Finn picked up his shredded pants and searched the material until he found his lighter in what had once been a back pocket. He lit some of the clothes on fire then tossed them onto one of the creatures. It immediately burst into flames. An eerie reddish-orange glow burned unnaturally bright and fast as the fire devoured the beast. Soon there would be nothing but ash. Thankfully the creatures burned with lightning speed, leaving no evidence behind.

"If you planned to have fun tonight, you should've called me." Gabriel's heavy boots thudded across the ground as he quickly strode through the warehouse. As

Guardian, it was his job to protect the Alpha of his pack at all times, but Finn didn't like to depend on anyone.

If he couldn't protect himself, how could anyone expect him to keep his pack safe? To maintain power in his region?

Finn didn't turn around as he lit the other creatures on fire. "Last time I checked, I'm still Alpha."

Gabriel sighed, a familiar sound. "You recruited me for a reason. To watch your back. What's the point of being Guardian if I have no one to *guard*?"

Finn snorted in response, but the truth was, he had recruited Gabriel for a very good reason. Years ago when Finn had killed his own hateful uncle and taken over the Stavros pack, there had been a few who would have seen him overthrown. For the most part he'd weeded out his enemies, but his uncle had been Alpha for over a thousand years and his archaic ideals were still strong with some.

Gabriel had been a loner until Finn found him. The other wolf had been passing through Biloxi and had jumped into the middle of a squabble between Finn and a few vampires who'd wanted to move in on his territory. Finn hadn't needed the help but ever since then they'd forged an unbreakable friendship.

Even if he technically didn't owe his friend an explanation, he gave one. "I didn't have time to call. I saw one of those things tailing a human female as she left the casino and tracked it. It left the female alone when it realized I was hunting it. Think it wanted to lure me into a trap."

When his friend didn't respond he grabbed the towel Gabriel extended and started wiping blood from his arms and sides. As Alpha, his healing speed was one of his gifts. His back and sides were sore but as he drew the towel away he could see the long slashes along his skin already mending. His medical kit was in his SUV but he decided not to bother patching himself up since the blood wasn't flowing anymore. After he finished, he took an extra set of clothes from Gabriel and quickly pulled on the dark sweater and jeans. They all carried extra clothes in their vehicles and Gabriel's assumption that he'd need them tonight was from previous experience. "How'd you know I'd be here anyway?"

"One of the girls at the front desk told me you'd left in a rush so I followed your scent. And you *did* have time to call. Or text." Gabriel shook his head as he picked up what was left of Finn's shredded shoes and fallen cell phone and keys. He tossed the ruined shoes into the fire.

Finn ignored Gabriel's last comment. "How'd you get here?" he asked as they exited the warehouse.

A bright three-quarter moon hung high in the sky, illuminating the dingy alley. There were a few empty cardboard boxes propped up against a rusted old Dumpster, but no signs of anyone, not even the homeless. There was another warehouse directly next to this one and it was also currently unused. Made sense for the demons to be hanging out here, but his pack would have to pay more attention to the area now. His SUV was still parked in the dark alley but he didn't see Gabriel's motorcycle anywhere.

"My bike's a block over. Wasn't sure if you were fighting anyone and didn't want to announce my presence if you needed backup. Besides, there's no way in hell I was parking my baby down here." He mock shuddered as he tossed the SUV keys to him.

Finn bit back a smile as he palmed the key fob. He briefly contemplated going back to the casino. But he had too much paperwork to catch up on and would be distracted there. "See ya back at the compound?"

Gabriel shook his head and grinned. "I'm going to head up to Howler's for a while."

Howler's was the club on the bottom floor of Finn's casino and since it was almost ten the place would just be getting busy. Even though he wasn't required to, Gabriel liked to help out security on the weekends. He'd never said it, but Finn knew he liked to let out his aggression on drunk shifters looking for a fight. "See ya tomorrow, then."

As Finn steered out of the alley, he glanced at his phone. Three missed calls from Spiro, one of the wolves he had running patrol at the compound tonight. Definitely not a good sign. He put in his hands-free earpiece and called him back.

Spiro picked up on the first ring. "Boss, we have a problem. There's a vampire here who says she knows you and needs to speak to you. She's injured two of our warriors and we've got her cornered by the edge of the house but...I get the feeling she's *letting* us corral her. I've never seen a vampire move so *fast*. She said you two have a history together."

Something tightened in his chest. Once he'd killed his uncle, Finn had searched for her for years; was *still* covertly searching for her. It seemed impossible, but... "What does she look like?"

"Long blonde hair, not very tall, *great* curves, grayish-purple vampire eyes—"

It hurt to breathe for a moment, but he made his throat work. "I'm on my way. Do not let her leave, but *no one* better injure her. They do, they die." He ended the call and gunned the engine. He was only minutes away but suddenly it seemed like an eternity stretched before him.

Finn knew only one vampire that fit that description and he hadn't seen the alluring woman in seventeen long years.

Lyra Marius.

The blonde-haired vampire with the unique grayish-violet eyes, sharp cheekbones and an adorable smattering of freckles over her nose had haunted his dreams for too long. She had an innocent quality about her that was refreshing. Having been raised to believe that all vampires were evil creatures it had surprised him when he'd first met her. Not a night went by that he didn't think—fantasize—about her. His cock hardened as her familiar image flooded his vision and he inwardly cursed his lack of self-control. With her, he'd never had much of it. Then again, neither had she.

After they'd broken up he'd tried to keep tabs on her but she'd fallen off the face of the earth. The vampire and werewolf communities didn't exactly communicate. Not openly anyway, and he hadn't been able to find out where she'd gone. He'd hoped she'd been living safely among her own kind. With her royal family. Protected and treasured as she should be. But after killing his uncle he'd heard a rumor she'd left her coven. He hadn't been able to validate it as truth or not. After that shred of gossip, there had been no word, not even a whisper of her, for the past seventeen years among *any* of his contacts. It was like she'd vanished.

It seemed too much to hope she was at his compound, but his heart rate increased just the same.

To see her again, to hold her again... His throat squeezed at the thought. Pushing her out of his life had been the hardest thing he'd ever done, but he'd had no choice.

Their affair had been short, intense, and completely forbidden. Vampires and werewolves were natural born enemies. They didn't sleep together, much less fall in love. Until he and Lyra had. But eventually he'd had to face reality.

If his uncle had discovered his relationship with a vampire, he'd have killed Lyra out of sheer spite. Even if Finn had broken from the pack and run away with Lyra—which he'd wanted to do—his uncle would have hunted them down and *still* had her killed out of pettiness. Not because he hated vampires—though he *had* despised them—but purely because of his hatred for Finn. From the moment Finn had been born, his uncle had made his life a living hell... Finn shook his head sharply.

Now was no time to dwell on the past. Vampires didn't just show up unannounced onto werewolf property. And vice versa. If Lyra was at his compound she was there for a reason and he needed to get to her before things escalated and someone got hurt.

CHAPTER TWO

Lyra's fangs lengthened as she stared at the four shifters in front of her. A couple of the animals pawed the ground as if they might lunge, but she wasn't too worried.

As a member of one of the royal families—exiled or not—she had the gift of flight. She couldn't soar for hundreds of miles or anything, but she could quickly move across city blocks when need be. If she had to flee, she would. But right now all she wanted was to talk to Finn. She hadn't even breached his compound.

After buzzing the main gate, they'd *let* her in. And then a couple of these young pups thought they could try to attack her? She gritted her teeth and snarled at them again.

Two of them took a few tentative steps back, but two stood their ground. With her back facing the sprawling mansion, she didn't have to worry about an attack from behind. She didn't sense anyone other than the four snarling pups in front of her. Lyra relied heavily on her extrasensory abilities, one that she shared with the shifters, and could usually scent those around her long before they got too close.

19

In an exclusive part of the historic city, Finn's compound was gated, expansive and very private. A huge iron fence and thick trees surrounded the acres of property and the Greek revival mansion directly behind her, but apparently no one inside was civilized. She supposed she could leave, but she didn't have anywhere else to go. After trying to call Finn's casino and being told he was unavailable, she'd decided to come directly to him. She only lived a few hours north of Biloxi so as soon as dusk had fallen, she'd driven straight there. Contacting him killed her inside, but she had no choice.

As she decided what move to make next, a shifter in human form raced across the lawn toward her and the growling shifters. "Back off!"

Immediately the other wolves fell back a few feet.

She tensed, waiting for another attempted attack.

"Finn is on his way. He doesn't want you to leave," the dark-haired man told her.

She glared at him. "If I'd *wanted* to leave, I could have at any time. In fact, I didn't have to come here in the first place. You werewolves have a lot to learn about manners."

"You're a vampire," the shifter said, as if that should explain everything.

"I buzzed your front gate." Dumbass. "I *tried* to announce myself in a civilized manner. I explained I needed to speak to your pack Alpha and you are the ones who attacked *me*. Do you really think if I'd planned a one-woman attack I would have buzzed you?" She ground her teeth together at their idiocy.

The man had the decency to look apologetic, but she didn't buy his sincerity. Nervously, he cleared his throat then motioned to the shifters to leave. Or at least she assumed that's what his abrupt hand gesture meant since the four animals walked away and disappeared among the trees on the property. He started to say something else but paused and turned his head.

She heard the faint sound too. Like the main gate opening. Despite her desire to stay calm, her heart rate increased. The shifter in front of her might think her a monster considering the way these animals had sought to attack her unprovoked, but she was very much alive. Blood flowed in her veins as much as it did in theirs. She just had an aversion to sunlight and a thirst for blood. Whether it was a genetic anomaly or because all supernatural beings were cursed by the gods as some said, she'd stopped caring long ago that she was different from the majority of the population. She was a bloodborn. A rare vampire who'd been born to this life, not turned, and she had every right to live just as anyone else.

Despite what a few angry wolves might think.

When the man in front of her started heading back across the expansive yard toward the winding driveway, she followed. Instead of using her gift, she walked.

Her four-inch heels sank into the grass with each step, but she was light on her feet and quickly surpassed the male shifter until she stood on the pavement waiting for the SUV barreling down the driveway. It jerked to a sudden halt, the vehicle shuddering. Even though she couldn't see inside it because of the tinted windows, she knew who was in there. Felt his presence in a bone deep, almost unexplainable kind of way. A mixture of nerves, excitement and flat out fear battled inside her, each one fighting for dominance and making her a little sick.

Finn jumped from the front seat—all six foot three of him. He didn't even bother to shut the door as he hurried toward her. His bright blue eyes seemed to bore right through her, as if he could see all her secrets. God help her if he actually could. "Lyra," he rasped out.

His voice was so familiar. So right, it made something long-forgotten burn inside her chest. The tingling sensation shoved jaggedly out to all her nerve endings, making her almost numb as she stared at him.

Finn Stavros. Former lover, one-time best friend, and the only man she'd ever given her heart to.

Why did he still have to be so damn sexy? So powerful? She swallowed hard, drinking in the sight of him like a blood-starved vamp. Her traitorous nipples tightened as her gaze tracked over his muscular body. It didn't matter that he had clothes on, she'd seen every inch of his delicious form.

For a brief moment, it was as if the past seventeen years had been stripped away. She'd been so young and sheltered when they first met. Technically at ninety she was still young for her species but she wasn't sheltered anymore and she definitely wasn't naïve. She blinked once and tried to banish the memory of meeting him but it refused to go away. After temporarily escaping her coven, intent on having a fun night out among humans, she'd stumbled directly into a shifter bar. Almost immediately she'd known she'd made a mistake.

A big one.

But she'd been frozen in shock, gazing around the bar that had looked so normal on the outside, but had been filled with supernatural beings on the inside. Being so sheltered she hadn't even known a place like that existed. Finn had taken one look at her and known *exactly* what she was. Lucky for her, he'd been the first to notice her and he'd quickly escorted her outside before any other shifters had scented her. He'd told her to get lost, but then he'd started talking to her and had made sure she'd gotten safely out of the area. He'd also given her a lecture on where she should go and where she shouldn't. It had been so endearing coming from the big shifter.

Then he'd done the most unexpected thing. He'd kissed her as if he couldn't stop himself. When he was through, he'd looked just as surprised as she'd felt. Swallowing hard at the memory, she touched her bottom lip, which was actually tingling. She still remembered his spicy taste. Even if she didn't want to, it somehow lingered there, taunting her. Reminding her of all she'd lost.

The other shifter cleared his throat and she jerked her gaze to the left. She'd forgotten they weren't alone.

He was staring at Finn. "Uh, boss?"

"Leave us," Finn growled softly.

When she turned back to him, she realized he hadn't taken his eyes off her. Even in her heels, the powerful man still towered over her. And he looked every bit as dominating as she remembered.

At one hundred and fifty years old he still looked the same physically. To a human he would appear about thirty. Tall, broad-shouldered, midnight black hair cropped close to his head, icy blue eyes and those arms... Her eyelids grew heavy as she watched his muscles flex lightly. The only difference was the darker edge to him now. He exuded a raw, primal quality that didn't exactly make her nervous, but she was *very* aware of it. Something dormant and annoyingly needy inside her flared to life. It wasn't something definitive she could put her finger on but he'd definitely changed since she'd last seen him and she liked what she saw.

"Why are you here, Lyra?" His deep, intoxicating voice jerked her back to reality.

A river of guilt and shame flooded her as his question registered. She shouldn't be staring at him and practically drooling. Not when her daughter had been taken. Not when she needed his help more than she'd ever needed anything. Bile rose in her throat at her stupid reaction to him. "I know you're Alpha of this region and... I need your help. My daughter has been kidnapped and I can't trust anyone else to help me."

CHAPTER THREE

Surprise registered on Finn's face but Lyra wasn't sure if it was because she'd just announced that she had a daughter or because she'd come to him for help. "What can I do?"

The moment he asked the question, she knew she'd done the right thing by coming to him. She'd heard that he'd killed his uncle and taken over a lot of the Southern werewolf territory so she'd been hopeful Finn still held a special place in his heart for her. Nonetheless, it stunned her that he was offering help so easily. Without even asking for details first. "You'll...help me? Just like that?"

His icy blue eyes flashed to a midnight color then reverted back so quickly she wondered if she'd imagined the change. Though she knew she hadn't. "Yes."

Lyra swallowed again. He'd probably hate her when he eventually learned the truth about what she'd been keeping from him, but for now, he didn't need to know. She could bear the guilt if it brought her daughter back home safely. Looking around, she knew there would be other people listening. Even if she couldn't see them, there were shifters around the yard and compound watching and listening. If his pack's reception of her was any indication of how they regarded vampires, she had no doubt they'd be curious about her. "Can we go somewhere private?"

He nodded and without pause, covered the few feet between them and scooped her up in his arms.

She stiffened in his hold. "I can walk." Or fly.

He just grunted so she didn't fight him as he hurried toward the house. Finn might be a lot of things but if he said he'd help her, he would. Which meant he had no intention of throwing her to his pack for dinner. A part of her, one that she almost hated, actually enjoyed his embrace. The way he was holding her close to his chest brought up long buried emotions.

He rushed through the front door and up a winding staircase and she got a quick glimpse of the interior. Downstairs a parlor room was on the left and what had probably once been a ballroom was on the right, but had been turned into a game room. The house was definitely historical, but everything from the overhead lighting to the dark, polished wood floors had been updated.

On the second floor he took her down a long hallway then stopped at the last door. The second they stepped inside she was immediately accosted with his scent. Piney, earthy, all Finn. She'd scented it in the house and on the grounds but in here it was more potent. At least she didn't smell another female in the room. An unwel-

DARKNESS AWAKENED | 29

come flare of jealousy sparked inside her at the thought of him mated to someone.

The second he set her on her feet, she nearly collapsed onto the end of his king-sized bed. She wasn't sure where to begin so she just started talking. "I'm not sure who's taken my daughter but I know they won't hurt her. Not yet anyway. Or...I don't think so." It was a hope she'd been desperately clinging to. "I think her kidnapping has something to do with this prophecy, but I could be wrong. God, this could be something else entirely." Panic hit her in the chest like a sharpened blade. What if she was wrong? What if Vega had been taken for other purposes? What if—

Finn knelt in front of her and took one of her hands, his eyes intent on hers. He stroked her palm with a callused thumb, the action soothing. "Let's clear a few things up. How old is your daughter? What's her name? And where was she taken from?"

"Vega is... fifteen." Lyra shaved off a year because she wasn't ready to tell Finn he was Vega's father. If she did, he'd have a million other questions and not only did they *not* have time for that, Lyra couldn't deal with his wrath. He would almost certainly decide to search for Vega on his own and exclude her. Considering she had no one else to turn to and he definitely had more resources than her... Lyra couldn't risk him shutting her out. Nope. Not an option. Her daughter was all that mattered. "She's very strong-willed and stubborn and…"

Her voice cracked but Finn squeezed her hand tighter. Finding her voice, she continued. "We fought bitterly. She wanted to go to New Orleans to meet up with some friends for a concert or something." Lyra mentally crossed her fingers at the lie. "But she's so young and I didn't want her to go on her own. It's not safe for anyone at that age to be traveling by themselves, much less a young vampire. She can walk in the daylight so while I was sleeping, she left anyway and when she was passing through Biloxi, she called me." That much was at least true. "She was scared and sorry for leaving and wanted me to come meet her when…" Lyra fought nausea for a moment. She had to get the words out now or she feared she'd break down. "I *heard* her being taken. She was screaming and terrified but Vega is smart. She told me it was a female and a male and that they were non-human before the line disconnected. As soon as dusk fell, I came straight here. I tried calling your casino but they wouldn't put me through to you."

He frowned but asked, "Do you have a picture of her with you?"

"I came straight here." A vague answer that wasn't exactly a lie.

"What's your daughter's phone number?"

After she rattled it off, he grabbed a pad and pen from his nightstand and jotted it down. "Whoever took her probably didn't bring her cell with them but if we can get a location on the phone itself, maybe we can figure out where exactly she was taken from and go from there."

"I know she was staying at a hotel on the beach." Lyra gave him the name of the hotel Vega had texted her about hours before her kidnapping and Finn wrote that down too.

"You said whoever took her hasn't hurt her. How do you know? And why isn't her father involved in finding her?" There was a distinctive bite to his question.

Lyra glanced at his chest because she couldn't bear to look him in the eyes. If she did, she feared he'd see straight through her. "Her father isn't involved in our lives." Not a lie. Not exactly the truth either, but she stomped the guilt back down. "I think she's been taken because of a prophecy. You've heard of Akkad?"

He nodded and those astute eyes of his darkened slightly. "Of course."

Every supernatural being knew of the old city. Akkad was once the capital of the Akkadian Empire, located in ancient Mesopotamia, and home to thousands of vampires. Human experts believed that roughly four thousand years ago an abrupt climate change helped in the demise of this city but she knew better. All supernatural beings did. Demons—since named Akkadian demons for their 'birth' place—wreaked havoc on the land after two greedy, self-serving priests made a deal with the devil. Literally.

In exchange for immortality they would help the devil open one of the gates in the Fertile Crescent, releasing his favorite children onto the earth. Unfortunately for these two priests, they didn't specify where they wanted to live out their immortal lives and got dropped directly into hell once they'd helped open the door. Demons were tricky bastards and if they could find a loophole, they would. Eventually a band of powerful vampires managed to close the door again, but not before an entire civilization had been wiped out and only the remnants of volcanic ash covered the razed ground.

"Then you know those monstrous creatures have been trying to get back out of hell ever since the door was shut." An unwelcome shudder snaked through her at the thought of Akkadian demons roaming the earth freely.

"Some already have." Finn's deep voice rumbled quietly in the giant room.

She jerked back in surprise. "What?"

"My pack and I have been dealing with Akkadian demons for the past month. Not too many, but enough that it's starting to cause problems."

She slowly digested his words. "There are only a few ways to open any of the gates of hell so if demons have escaped, then..."

"It's likely from human sacrifices—it's the easiest way." He finished the thought for her.

Of course there were other options in addition to human sacrifice. The sacrifice of a dragon shifter would obliterate any door to hell, not just open it, but no one had seen a dragon in millennia and Lyra doubted they even existed anymore. Someone could use a first-class religious relic such as the bones from a martyr or saint in *addition* to a blood sacrifice, but true relics were hidden away by churches and guarded very carefully. Just like with a human blood sacrifice, that one was only a temporary way to unlock a gateway.

Even *huge* amounts of human sacrifice would only let out a couple at a time. Not enough to be worth anyone's while. But if someone had started letting them escape *now*, it only solidified what Lyra thought. What she didn't want to think about. There was another option. One based on a prophecy that vampires had guarded since Akkad was destroyed.

"There's an ancient prophecy among my people. We've kept it guarded for almost four thousand years. I never thought much about it until..." Until she'd gotten pregnant with a shifter's baby. But she didn't voice that. She couldn't. It was one of the reasons she'd kept Vega's birth a secret from so many people. She'd reveal to Finn only what she had to about the prophecy. "A vampire named Kush prophesied that fifteen years after two powerful lines created life, the sun would go dark across the entire planet in the middle of the day. When that happens, the progeny of those two lines will have the power to completely open the gates of hell with their blood and spill terror onto the planet once again. In five days there's a solar eclipse and Vega is the only blood-born to survive a vampire birth since...me."

"Your daughter is the youngest blood-born vampire?"

Tightly, Lyra nodded. That was true but not everything she'd told him was. The prophecy actually stated that in her sixteenth year, the only hybrid vampire-wolf blood-born would have the ability to open and close one of the portals to hell with her blood. But if Lyra admitted her daughter's real age and the fact that Vega was a blood-born hybrid, Finn would know the truth. Yeah, so not going to happen.

"And her father is—"

"*Not* involved." She didn't even want to go there. The continuous lying made her sick but she'd do anything to save her daughter. Vega was everything to Lyra. She'd lay down her life to keep her daughter from just one hour of harm. If Finn knew the truth, he might try to punish her or exclude her from the search. And that wasn't happening.

A deep growling sound rattled in his chest but he didn't comment further. "What about your brother? Why isn't he helping?"

"I haven't seen Claudius in years." Seventeen to be exact. Claudius had kicked her out of the coven the moment he'd discovered she was pregnant with Finn's baby. An abomination, he'd called Vega. The things he'd called Lyra had been much worse. She'd been prepared for his scorn, but not for him to kick her out hours before sunrise. Lyra's heart ached as she thought of the terrible words they'd exchanged and how utterly alone she'd been back then. She'd made human friends in the years since she'd struck out on her own, but she still missed living with her people.

"Where have you been living—"

His question was cut off by the low buzzing sound of her phone. Feeling almost frantic, she retrieved it from her pants' pocket. The caller ID said 'unknown'. Irrational hope flared inside her that this might be Vega. "Hello?"

"Mo...Mom?" Vega's voice was slightly slurred. Simultaneous relief and pain flooded Lyra.

"Honey? Where are you? Are you okay?" Turning away from Finn, she pressed the phone tighter against her ear, as if that could somehow bring her closer to her daughter.

"I'm...okay. They havensh hurt...me."

"*Who* hasn't hurt you? Where are you?" The claws on her free hand unsheathed as she fought to breathe. If anyone had hurt her daughter—

"Nope. You're not getting that answer," a female voice said in a creepy sing-song tone. It was almost as if the voice was being modified by a machine. "Your daughter is currently being fed and clothed and kept in nice living quarters. If you do something stupid, like try to involve *anyone* or come looking for her, that will change."

Cold seeped into Lyra's veins, slow and utterly painful. "So you expect me to do nothing?"

"I expect you'll do the smart thing to keep your daughter alive." Her voice was now razor sharp.

"Why was she talking like that? What have you done to her?" Lyra could see Finn out of the corner of her eye moving closer but she closed her eyes, needing to block him out.

"We're keeping her sedated. If anything, we're doing her a favor. We only need her for her blood and when we're done taking what we need, we'll let her go. Leave this thing alone and your daughter will be back in your arms after the eclipse five days from now."

"I want to talk to—"

The line went dead. So much raw fury and pain lanced through her that she shook with it. Still sitting on the edge of the bed, she opened her eyes to find Finn staring intently at her. "Did you hear that?" she asked, her voice uneven.

He nodded. "Do you have any idea who 'we' is?"

She shook her head because she didn't trust her voice and she didn't want to break down now. It wouldn't do her daughter any good.

"It sounds like you're right. They're planning on using her blood to completely open the door when the time is right. Human sacrifices aren't a long term option and..." Finn looked hard at her for a long moment, as if searching for the right words. "I don't say this to be harsh, but you know they'll kill her after the eclipse?"

Lyra snorted loudly as she stood. No kidding. Once they'd opened a door they'd have no use for her. She wasn't going to stand idly by, despite what that woman had said. That had never been an option. And the fact that the female who'd called had seemed to know that she was already searching for help bothered Lyra. The call seemed unnecessary unless someone *knew* she'd come to Finn. And she hadn't told a soul where she was going. "There are a few hours of darkness still left. I can't stay cooped up here. We've got to do something *now*." Her daughter was alive. Lyra kept repeating the words over in her head. Vega was alive and whoever had taken her definitely needed her alive until the eclipse. Five days. She would get her daughter back before then or die trying.

Finn shook his head slightly as if he was going to say no. She was ready to argue but he eventually gave her a short nod. "I know the owner of the hotel your daughter was staying at. We can search the room. It's likely been cleaned by now but maybe I'll pick up a scent I recognize. Maybe you will too."

The heavy weight on her chest lifted a fraction. She knew it was improbable that they'd find anything but she needed to be where Vega had been. They had to explore every option. "Let's go then."

The trip to the hotel had turned up nothing. Lyra wasn't surprised but she was irrationally disappointed. The room Vega stayed in only had the faintest trace of her daughter's scent left. Her daughter smelled like moonlight and roses. From the moment she'd been born, the scents had struck Lyra so deeply. Every time she looked at her daughter she felt that innate happiness pouring off her. And someone had taken her away.

Right now Lyra wanted to strike out at someone. Anything to momentarily dull the pain growing inside her. Finn had been so quiet after they'd left the hotel room.

When he looked at her she saw pity in his gaze. Which only made her want to slice him up. Irrational? Yes. She just didn't care. Part of her knew that if she didn't get a hold of her baser vampiric instincts to kill she'd go mad and strike out at anyone who got in her way.

As they drove back to Finn's home in silence, a chasm seemed to be forming between them. Normally she didn't mind silence but the quiet seemed to stretch endlessly. It gave her too much time to think. Too much time to dwell on 'what if' questions running through her head. Like 'what if she didn't find her daughter in five days?' or 'what if Finn discovered her lie before they found Vega?'

She fought her urge to look at Finn, but nothing could block out her peripheral vision. While she ached so badly inside, she still couldn't deny her awareness of the tall and powerful shifter. She might hate and want to ignore it, but it had been like that the first time she'd met him. As if something inside her had woken up the instant they'd locked gazes. With his Mediterranean heritage his skin was a gorgeous olive tone. If anything he was even darker than he'd been years ago. The differences between his darker skin and her pale body had always been so erotic to her when they'd been naked and tangled up together. Longing punched into her with a surprising jolt as she remembered what he'd been able to do with the long fingers currently wrapped around the steering wheel.

As another thought occurred to her, she tensed and asked, "Is it going to cause problems with me staying in your room?"

He glanced at her with his eyebrows lifted. "Why would it?"

She shrugged, hating the dark side of her that wanted to start a fight with him just to take her mind off Vega's absence. "I'm just surprised you're not mated yet...or at least seeing someone." She knew him well enough that he wouldn't have let her stay in his room if he was involved with someone, safety issues or not. And any sane she-wolf wouldn't have put up with another female staying in her intended mate's room. She-wolves were just as territorial as vampires.

"I'm surprised you're not either." His response threw her. He hadn't answered, not that she'd actually given him a question. And she didn't miss the slight questioning note in his voice, though she chose to ignore it.

She pursed her lips, unsure what to say. Of course she wasn't mated. After being with Finn, other males paled in comparison. And she hated that about him as much as she still desired him. Just being around him and that familiar male scent reminded her of all the sensuous things they'd done together. How his mouth had covered every inch of her body in teasing kisses. The only good thing about that was that it proved to be an actual distraction to her inner turmoil.

As they neared the Biloxi Bay Bridge, he slowed and turned into a parking lot next to one of the casinos right on the water. Instead of heading for the parking garage attached to the casino, he continued driving across the deserted lot and headed for the water. "What are you doing?"

Finn briefly turned those ice blue eyes in her direction. "There are still a couple hours left until sunrise. You're tense and need to let out the rage I can sense coming from you."

Something akin to annoyance burst inside her. "And how do you plan on helping me get out my rage?"

He gave her a sharp look that said he knew what she assumed he'd meant. Then he nodded toward the bridge, now looming on their left. "There's a walkway that connects from Biloxi to Ocean Springs. It doesn't happen often but I've caught a few of the demons lurking on the bridge after dusk. Most humans don't venture here at night but if they do and get attacked, they don't have anywhere to go unless they want to jump into the bay."

From her vantage point that was a pretty high drop even from the lowest point, which appeared to be about fifty feet up. The highest could be closer to a hundred feet.

"So...you want to hunt some of the demons?" Lyra's hands automatically clenched into fists as her body prepared for a fight. Killing some of the very monsters who were indirectly the cause of Vega's kidnapping sounded perfect.

He shrugged and for a brief moment his gaze flicked to her chest. "I can see the outline of the blade you're carrying under your jacket. I'm assuming you know how to use it?"

When she nodded, his lips pulled into a thin line, as if he didn't like that idea. "When did you start carrying weapons?"

"Seventeen years ago." Uncaring what he made of her statement, she turned from him and got out of the vehicle. The salty ocean air instantly enveloped her senses.

She heard a soft growl before she slammed the door shut. Self-consciously she played with the zipper of her lightweight black jacket, wondering if he'd noticed her gun. Oh yes, she had a gun too. As a single female vampire traveling alone, she was always prepared. Considering her vampire strength, agility and incredible speed it was unlikely she'd have to use her weapons on a human intent on doing her harm, but there were a lot of non-human predators out there.

The gravel from the unpaved parking lot crunched under her flat, steel-toed boots. It had been a while since she'd gone out hunting, but she hadn't forgotten how. Even though she'd been sheltered from the moment she was born she'd trained often. And after Vega's birth she'd picked up some new tricks in an effort to better defend herself and her daughter.

Voices of humans on their way to gamble from the parking garage carried on the wind. The noise of cars and trucks zooming down the highway next to the enclosed walkway on the bridge grew louder as they approached it. Despite the city lights, she could see a few twinkling stars above the ocean.

She and Finn walked in silence across the bridge. A few cabin cruisers and even a tiny aluminum boat passed through the calm intracoastal waterway under them. Over a mile and a half and no humans in sight so they turned around. The energy and anger humming through her had faded a little, but not much. She hated feeling so helpless where her daughter was concerned. And her annoying awareness of Finn didn't help her guilt.

On their return trek, she froze as they neared the point they'd started. She'd never actually seen an Akkadian demon—just rough drawings from some old texts—but she knew what she was staring at. The skin that stretched over the large humanoid creature's body was reptilian. It had hollowed out cheeks and glowing eyes.

The clawed hands and feet added to the creature's already horrific appearance. If she had to guess, it was about seven feet tall.

Before Lyra could think of anything to say, another, smaller female creature appeared from behind the male. She could tell the differences in their sex because they had similar body parts as humans. If for some reason she had any doubt what they were, they absolutely stank. They put off a nasty sulfuric scent that raked against her over sensitive vampiric senses.

Finn immediately took a step forward, partially blocking her body.

Though she was touched by his protectiveness, she ignored him and kept her gaze on the first creature hovering by the entrance to the walkway of the bridge. Its eyes had a yellow tint a little lighter than a harvest moon. The color was unusual and creepy.

Ballsy creature, Lyra thought. Another more potent scent on the breeze caught her nostrils. She glanced over the edge of the bridge onto the gravel parking lot below. There were two more of them.

Since they were close to the end of the walkway it would only be about a ten foot drop from the last stretch of the bridge to the ground. She made a decision. "Two more below us. I'll get them. You take those." She motioned to the male and female in front of them. Without waiting for Finn's response, Lyra unzipped her jacket and unsheathed her twelve inch blade as she jumped over the edge.

Her jacket flapped lightly in the wind, but the demons didn't see or hear her until it was too late. With her knife outstretched, she sliced through one demon's neck straight to the bone. Thick red fluid sprayed everywhere and a sulfuric scent permeated the air.

The thing hit the ground about the same time her feet did. The other creature snarled as it rushed her. Sharp claws sliced through her upper arm as it grabbed her and slung her to the ground.

The strength behind that hold surprised her. But not enough to make her tuck tail and run. Jumping to her feet she let her fangs and the claws on one hand extend. A low growl built in her throat as she began to circle the creature.

It dove at her again with no apparent thought to its survival. With its head low, it tried to barrel into her chest.

Using all the strength in her legs she propelled herself upward, jumping completely over it. In the air she turned and came back down hard on the creature. Her free hand dug into its shoulder for a firm grip while she raised the blade with her right hand. She drew it up high and to the left then slashed hard back down in a giant arc to sever the head.

Instinctively she jerked back as more putrid fluid sprayed her. She raised her arm so that it missed her face.

As the body hit the ground next to its fallen companion, something unexpected happened. The demon with the half-severed head began to move.

"Son of a..." Moving lightning fast she jumped on it and finished what she'd started. The razor sharp weapon completed its job with one lethal pass.

Pushing up, she tensed as she heard slight movement behind her. Before she'd turned completely around, however, she relaxed. Finn's earthy scent was unmistakable.

"You okay?" Real concern laced his voice as he raced toward her, his boots almost soundless.

She nodded, her adrenaline still pumping. "Did you get the other two?"

"Yeah. You sure you're all right?" He took another step toward her and she instantly backed away. She couldn't take his concern right now. Not when she was this edgy.

She quickly stripped off her blood soaked jacket, knowing she wouldn't be wearing it again.

Finn extended his hand. Unsure what he meant, she handed him her jacket. In one tug, he ripped it in two. After lighting each piece on fire, he threw them on the dead creatures.

Lyra watched in fascination as they burst into flames so quickly. They were already turning to ash as she and Finn walked away.

"I already got the other two on the bridge. There won't be anything left of them soon."

"They burn just like...vampires." It was a little disturbing to have anything in common with the monstrous creatures.

Finn grunted in agreement. When they reached the SUV, he opened the back hatch and unzipped a duffle bag. "I always have extra clothes so if you want to change I'll give you privacy." He didn't look at her as he spoke but his thoughtfulness moved her.

Her dark sweater had been covered by her jacket but it was ripped where she'd been grabbed. Her own blood had dried on it and her pants had traces of the sulfuric scented blood on them. It might not be visible but she could smell it. Frowning, she scanned the rest of her body. As she wiped her boots off with a rag, she asked, "How did you stay so clean killing those others?"

He shrugged. "Practice. We've been killing these things the past couple weeks."

"One of them grabbed me and it was strong. Like *really* strong." She decided to keep the pants she had on since they might run into more of the creatures but her ripped sweater needed to go. If they ran into humans it wouldn't do to stand out.

"Some are stronger than others, and some only seem to have limited reasoning skills."

She nodded in agreement, but didn't say anything else. After finding a long-sleeved T-shirt small enough to fit, she stripped off her torn sweater so that she was just wearing a bra.

Next to her Finn sucked in a breath. "Damn it, Lyra. I didn't realize you'd been wounded." He covered the short distance between them and lifted her arm so that it was outstretched.

She started to tug away but his eyes narrowed. "I'm cleaning your arm."

Even though she didn't like standing in front of him feeling so exposed and she definitely didn't like him taking care of her—that brought back way too many memories—she waited while he opened the first aid kit. Expertly he swiped and cleaned her wound which was already healing, and would be fine by the end of the night. Then he carefully wrapped a bandage around her arm. She barely felt any pain with his deft fingers gliding over her skin. All she experienced was heat and desire racing through her. That was the most unnerving thing of all. She shouldn't be feeling *anything* other than agony right now. Guilt and worry for Vega cut through her worse than her physical wound, but this longing for him was unnerving.

She knew part of it was biological. There was just something about him that had always called to her. But she also knew the memories she carried of them together weren't helping things. With the not-quite-full moon overhead and few visible stars over the glistening water, the vivid vision of their first time together flickered in and out of her mind. She tried to banish it, but it was fighting for dominance over everything else.

The oversized quilt he'd laid out. The incredibly bright moon that night. The giant pond with the weeping willow giving them ultimate privacy. His mouth and gentle hands as he'd brought her to climax more than once before he'd ever entered her—

"You sure you're okay?" His voice was raspy and uneven as he stepped back and closed the kit.

Breathing hard, she looked up to find him eyeing her with a mix of warring emotions in his expression. In that moment she was very thankful he couldn't read her mind. Guilt and lust seemed to be the most prevalent in his gaze. Her own heart rate increased as his blue eyes darkened and roved over her exposed flesh.

"I'm fine." Physically maybe, but inside was another story. She thought she'd been ready to face him, but being near him after so many years apart had her off kilter. She was wearing a bra, but it didn't matter. He stared at her as if he could see *everything*. As if he was remembering what he'd seen so many times before.

She felt completely bare under that heated gaze. And it was her own fault. She couldn't believe she'd just casually stripped off her sweater in front of him. To shifters, nudity was no big deal and for the most part, it wasn't to vampires either. It wasn't as if she ran around naked for the fun of it, but she was old enough that she felt comfortable in her own skin.

But that wasn't why she'd casually stripped. Like an idiot, she hadn't been thinking. Talking with him had felt familiar. *Way too familiar.* Once upon a time they hadn't just been lovers, they'd been friends. Hell, he'd been the best friend she'd ever had. She'd been trapped by her family's rules and regulations, rarely allowed to leave the coven unless she snuck out. They'd carried on their secret affair for six months, sneaking away anytime they could to see each other. And each time they'd ended up naked.

Shivering as memories accosted her, she turned her back to him. As she started to pull the shirt on, his callused hand stroked along the length of her spine.

Slow, seemingly casual, but she knew better. Power and dominance hummed in that gentle touch and sent a shower of goose bumps rippling over her skin. Instinctively she clenched her legs together as that long-forgotten ache built deep inside her. This was definitely the wrong time and the wrong place. She wanted to shake herself at the way he made her body come alive, but couldn't do anything about it.

"Lyra." One word. That was all he said. But her name on *his* lips made her weak and stupid. He sounded so damn desperate and out of character from the man she remembered.

Against her better judgment, she turned to face him. The need and raw hunger in his eyes not only made her stupid, it turned her knees to mush. She swallowed hard and opened her mouth to say something.

Anything semi-intelligent.

Nothing came out.

He growled low in his throat as his head descended toward hers. All coherent thought and reasoning dissipated the instant their lips touched.

Heat and fire swept through her as their tongues clashed. She felt his kiss bone deep as vivid memories resurfaced. Memories she wanted no part of. A pull and desire for him she'd long-since buried erupted from somewhere inside her, a place she'd almost forgotten existed.

A moan built in her throat when his hand came up to the back of her neck and gripped her tight. He held onto her so hard, as if he was afraid she'd bolt. Which would be the sane and logical thing to do. But she couldn't find enough self-control or self-preservation to do that.

Not now.

Not when Finn's other skilled hand skimmed her bare stomach and worked its way up to her covered breast. In an instant, he pulled one of the lace cups down and thumbed her nipple.

Leaning back against the open hatch, she welcomed him into her embrace as she wrapped her legs around him. She clutched his shoulders as he began stroking over her hardening nipple the same way his tongue stroked her tongue.

Rolling her hips against him, she savored the feel of his hard length. Even with their clothing as a barrier, the sensation of having him so close was scorching and combustible.

When he reached around to unhook her bra, he suddenly froze at a buzzing sound. Her eyes flew open as she felt the vibration coming from his back pocket against her calf.

Before he could say anything she removed her legs from around him and shoved at his chest. Guilt swept over her like a brutal tsunami. Even those few brief seconds were too much time wasted. Time she should be doing...something.

He growled and angrily answered his phone while she turned away from him and tugged the T-shirt on. Without looking at him, she made her way to the front of the vehicle. The sun would be up soon and they needed to get back to his place. She'd never cared about her inability to walk in the daylight until now.

Until her daughter needed her most.

"I hate coming to this place," Gabriel muttered as he put the SUV into park next to a sleek black car that probably cost half a million dollars.

"Me too." Finn stepped out into the sunshine. Gravel crunched under his feet as he made his way to the nondescript warehouse that most humans probably assumed was a place for storage. Located near a local marina, this warehouse looked like a dozen others in the vicinity all used to store RVs and boats. Of course it was sound-proofed and very different inside.

Even if Lyra had been able to come with him to this place, Finn wouldn't have brought her to Bo Broussard's nightclub for supernatural creatures. Well, it wasn't exactly a nightclub since Bo, the half-demon half-human, kept it open practically 24/7.

As Finn and Gabriel reached the simple white door—a slight shade lighter than the actual building—it swung open before he was able to knock. Finn glanced up at one of many discreet video cameras, knowing Bo was probably watching.

The man—or ghoul, Finn realized as he took in the dark ring of red around his irises—who opened the door stepped back and nodded at both of them. "Bo's in his office. Said you could go back."

Finn grunted as he and Gabriel stepped into a wide open space that housed the main bar. There were no windows in the two-story building. Just a bar that served *anything* any supernatural creature might want, a giant dance floor, muted music filtering in from unseen speakers, a few roped off booths with heavy curtains drawn back, and about a dozen rooms lay beyond a red door to their right. Behind that door were things Finn would prefer to never see. He knew Bo catered to a BDSM crowd but the half-demon never caused trouble and had a neutral territory for all creatures. Nothing non-consensual happened in here. It was fairly common knowledge that about eighty years ago Bo's human mother had been taken against her will by a demon—and Bo had been born not long afterward. So whatever his faults or proclivities, the guy respected females.

Since this was Finn's territory he could kick Bo out of town, but Bo had never given him a reason to. He just hoped the half-demon would be able to provide the information he was looking for.

Striding across the open floor to another simple white door, he opened it into a hallway. There were a few doors to choose from but he knew which one was Bo's. The last one. After knocking once out of courtesy, he and Gabriel entered to find Bo sitting behind a giant desk typing away on his computer.

The half-demon flicked his purple gaze their way. The color of his irises matched the purple streaks running through Bo's dark hair. Finn had no clue what color his real eyes were because they were different every time he saw him—which wasn't often.

"What can I do for you?" Bo asked, turning from his computer and motioning to the two seats in front of the desk.

Finn and Gabriel remained standing. "What do you know about Akkadian demons?"

The half-demon's light brown cheeks flushed an angry red as he leaned back in his chair. "I consider myself neutral, but those monsters...I killed one last night attempting to attack one of my bartenders as she was leaving."

"Do you know why they're escaping—or being released—now?" Finn asked, unwilling to divulge the information about the prophecy Lyra had told him.

Bo's freakish eyes narrowed a fraction. "It might have something to do with a prophecy."

Finn felt Gabriel's eyes on him, but he ignored his friend. "*You* know about the prophecy?"

Bo nodded. "I was involved with a very chatty vampire a few decades ago. Librarian. Liked to talk even while we uh...never mind."

At the word vampire, Finn believed Bo did know about the prophecy. It bothered him that Lyra had never told him about it when they were together but considering the way he'd left her, he couldn't exactly get too pissed about it. "If you know about that, then have you heard anything about a teenage blood-born being kidnapped in town over the past couple days?"

Frowning as he crossed his arms over his chest, Bo shook his head. "No... There was a kidnapping here? You mean *in* Biloxi?"

Finn nodded.

Bo's frown deepened. "I haven't heard about any kidnapping...I always thought the prophecy was bullshit, but there have been underworld rumblings about the Akkadians being freed soon." He spoke the word Akkadians as if it were a curse. "I just never thought that kind of mating was possible."

Finn sharpened his gaze. Blood-borns were rare, but they weren't *unheard* of. Lyra was proof enough of that. Unwilling to comment more on the subject to a half-demon he barely trusted, he nodded once at Gabriel who stepped toward the door. "I'm searching for the kidnapped girl and it's *very* personal. If I hear you had anything to do with it or know anything about it and didn't tell me, I'll burn this place to the ground with you still in it," he said quietly.

Bo's eyes widened and though it was slight, Finn scented a trickle of fear roll off the other man. "I swear I know nothing about this but I'll put out feelers. Just because I'm part demon doesn't mean I want those bastards roaming the earth. I *like* my life. They'll just bring chaos and destruction if they're all freed."

Finn hated threatening anyone but if this prophecy was true, he didn't have the luxury of being diplomatic. It was why he'd come in person as opposed to calling Bo. By showing up he made all the statement he needed to. "You have my number. Call me if you hear anything."

Once they were outside Gabriel spoke for the first time. "I believe him."

"Me too." Which was almost unfortunate. If he'd been lying it might have given them a decent lead. Finn had already called most of his out of town contacts and anyone he could think of who might know something. If they could locate the door letting the creatures out before the eclipse they could cut off whoever was doing it at the knees and stop them from opening the door fully. It would also lead them to Lyra's daughter.

Lyra had a daughter. He kept trying to wrap his mind around *that*. The thought of her with someone else, having a child with someone else...it raked at his insides like sharp silver daggers. If he'd never kicked her out of his life she'd have been only his. No one would have ever touched the woman who belonged with him. Knowing he had to keep those emotions on lockdown, he tried to shove his feelings away. Unfortunately that lid had popped and he had a feeling he'd never be able to compartmentalize this shit again.

Taking the SUV keys from Gabriel, Finn slid into the driver's seat. Right now the need to control something was overwhelming. As he started driving he realized he was headed back to his pack's place. He'd given strict orders to leave Lyra alone while she slept so he wasn't worried anyone would try to harm her. She could take care of herself as he'd seen firsthand last night. But being apart from her now was almost impossible to bear. It had taken every ounce of self-control he possessed to walk away from her once. Now that she was in his life again, he felt that magnetic pull to her. Only it was stronger this time. And it wasn't just sexual. She evoked too many emotions inside him, making him feel off balance and not in control of his wolf. A dangerous thing.

He was so damn tempted to tell her that he'd searched for her, that he'd been searching for her from the moment he'd killed his uncle. That he desperately wanted her back in his life. But he knew she wouldn't believe him. No, he needed to show her that she could trust him again. Show her how much he still cared for her before he told her the truth.

"We could check out a few other places," Gabriel said quietly.

Finn didn't respond because he knew what his friend *wasn't* saying out loud.

His friend continued after a long pause. "She's a vampire."

"I don't care." And he didn't. He never had.

"Neither do I, but you know not everyone will accept her."

"I'm just helping out an old friend." Even as he said the words he knew they weren't true.

Gabriel snorted. "And I'm the fucking Easter Bunny. If you mate with her—"

"I'm helping Lyra find her daughter and trying to stop this scourge of demons from escaping." Not that he hadn't *thought* about taking Lyra as his mate a thousand times. He knew the truth, however. Could see the barely veiled anger in her gaze when she looked at him. If she'd had anyone else to turn to, she would have. He knew that.

He hated it.

But that didn't mean he wouldn't try to push his way back into her life. Subtlety had never been his forte. She might dislike him but she was still attracted to him. That kiss last night proved it. While he planned to do everything in his power to save Lyra's daughter, it didn't mean he couldn't try to win Lyra back at the same time. He had to prove he was a male who would stand by her side no matter what.

After talking to a couple packmates and dealing with pack business that just wouldn't wait, Finn found himself standing in front of his bedroom door, the key in the lock. He'd instructed Lyra to lock it when he left and now he was rooted to the spot. Like some randy cub.

When he heard some of his packmates' voices trailing up the stairs, he flicked the lock open and stepped inside. No need to let anyone see him standing outside his own room like a hesitant puppy.

Not the type of message an Alpha should be sending. He had some pride.

The blackout curtains had been pulled over the windows and he'd ordered the external shutters drawn, but the small lamp on his nightstand was on. Lyra wasn't on the bed, but on the floor next to it sitting with her legs crossed and her head in her hands. She moved slightly at the sound of him entering, but didn't look at him.

He stayed by the door, not wanting to disturb her, even though everything inside him wanted to pull her into his arms and comfort her. "Lyra?"

When she looked up, the dark circles he'd seen under her eyes yesterday were even more pronounced and she had dried streaks of pink across her cheeks. The realization that she'd been crying was like a body blow.

He'd crossed the room and knelt in front of her before he was aware he'd moved. Reaching out, he brushed back a few strands of her blonde hair and tucked them behind her ear. He let his hand linger on her tear-stained cheek. That grayish-violet gaze of hers didn't waver from his, her pain and weariness so clear he could drown in it.

"Have you slept at all?" The question came out rough and uneven.

She shook her head and a couple more pink tears streamed down her cheeks. "I keep seeing Vega's face and hearing one of our last conversations play over in my head. I was so angry that she'd disobeyed me. Since she was born it's just been the two of us..." She paused and for a moment something dark passed over her features, as if she hadn't meant to tell him that.

Finn had already put out feelers to find out who the hell her daughter's father was. He was going to find out exactly who'd abandoned them—and make the bastard pay. The thought of Lyra raising a daughter by herself made him ache for her in a way he hadn't known was possible. Something hollow settled in his chest.

"When she turned... around the time of her last birthday we developed a psychic connection that manifests when I'm sleeping. She can link with me when she's awake or asleep, but I have to be sleeping. I just want to rest and maybe reach out to her. Just for a few minutes." Her voice cracked on the last word, a pink tear rolling down her cheek.

"*What?*" The teenager had psychic abilities? He knew Lyra didn't so he assumed the psychic gift was paternal. Just who the hell was this girl's father?

Lyra nodded, her face still grim as she swiped at the tear. "She's...a special vampire. Her father doesn't have psychic abilities that I'm aware of. I think her blossoming abilities have something to do with the combination of her bloodline. I just don't know and there's no one to ask, no one to help us figure it out. I have no freaking control over the connection." She sighed, the sound weary. "I just know it's only happened when I've been sleeping. The first time she told me it was by accident."

Sucking in a deep breath, Lyra's body began to slightly shake as she continued. "I'd give anything to be able to connect with her now. I yelled at her the first time she called me from the road and then the next time we spoke she was so scared because she was by herself in a new city. What if we don't find her? What if—" Her voice broke off and she shook her head, obviously unable to continue.

Finn felt out of his depth with Lyra—always had—but one thing between them hadn't faded. That attraction he'd once had for her was a scorching flame and he knew she felt the same. He might not have the right words—and even he knew now was not the time to ask more questions—but he could help her sleep and connect with her daughter.

Cupping her face, he brought his mouth down on hers. There was nothing gentle in his kiss because this wasn't about gentleness. She needed rest if she wanted to work together on finding her daughter. Right now, he could give her physical release and hopefully cause her to sleep. It had always worked in the past. She always fell sound asleep after the intense sex between them.

His tongue stroked in her mouth for a bare moment before she pushed at his shoulder and drew her head back. There was anger and hunger in her eyes, the battle raging so clearly it floored him. "What are you doing?"

"You need sleep," he said softly.

"You kissing me isn't going to help. Besides, I'm fine." Her voice was hoarse and her eyes had a glassy sheen, partially from her earlier tears but mainly from exhaustion.

That haunted look was too much to bear. "You're not and you're not doing your daughter any favors by staying awake."

"I can't sleep!" Scrubbing a hand over her face, she looked away. "I've tried," she muttered, her voice filled with disgust.

He pulled her chin back around so that she faced him. "I'm going to help you sleep and you're going to let me and just maybe you'll find that psychic connection again." There was no room for argument in his voice and when he crushed her mouth with his once again, this time she didn't fight him.

Instead she let out a strangled moan as she wrapped her arms around him, fiercely clawing at his back. For an instant he contemplated moving them to the bed, but selfish bastard that he was, he didn't want to risk her changing her mind. He wanted to taste her, bring her pleasure and more than anything, remove those shadows from under her eyes. Or at least dull them for a little while.

He couldn't heal any of her inner agony. Only finding her daughter could do that. But he could make her sleep.

Reaching between them, he shoved at her tiny black sleep shorts covered with glow-in-the-dark red vampire lips. If it had been any other situation he'd have laughed at the adorable nightwear but now he could only think about Lyra's pleasure. And feeling the heat between her legs was freeing his most animalistic side in a way she'd only ever done to him.

Once she was free of the shorts, he cupped her mound while still kissing her. She rolled her hips once against his hand and when he thrust two fingers inside her sheath without warning, she bucked wildly.

Normally he would have worked up to this. Taken his time and kissed and teased every single inch of her sweet body. Not now.

She was wet, but it wasn't nearly enough. Drawing his fingers out of her, he shuddered at the feel of her inner walls clamping around him. Being with her like this was almost torture. He might want a second chance with her, but deep down he knew she'd never give him one.

And he couldn't blame her. When he'd left her, he hadn't been cruel, but he had been clear that they had no future together—and maybe he had been harsh. It had been the only way to keep her out of his life.

Keep her safe. Keep her *alive.*

A dark weight settled in his gut but it had no place there at the moment. Mentally shaking himself, he inhaled her familiar sweet scent and was swept back to almost two decades ago.

When he nibbled along her jaw she let out a tiny moan that tore through him, making his entire body tense. What he wouldn't give to strip off his clothes and push more than his fingers into her.

Remembering how tight she'd been, how perfectly his cock had fit inside her made him a little crazy. "Tell me what you want," he murmured next to her ear, inhaling her scent. Her scent had always reminded him of caramel and raspberries. So much so that he couldn't eat either food without thinking of her.

"Make me sleep. Make me forget," she panted out, a frantic, desperate note in her voice.

Moving his way to her collarbone, he didn't bother removing the formfitting black T-shirt. He shredded the front until her breasts were displayed. What little brain function he'd been clinging to dissipated at the sight of her perfect dark pink nipples.

He'd sucked and kissed them so many times in the past, but seeing her now splayed out before him made something primal inside him wake up. The part of him he'd had to bury in order to survive the last seventeen years. There had been no one for him since her. The thought of taking another woman to his bed had been wrong on so many levels. He'd tried to kill his dreams and fantasies of her, but they'd always crept into his sub-conscious. Having her underneath him now was like sensory overload.

This might be about her right now, but she was still *his*. His brain and purely animal side clawed at him, tell-ing him to claim her. To plunge inside her and rake his teeth along the gentle slope of her neck. To extend his canines and pierce that delicate skin, letting everyone know she belonged to him.

Shutting down that part of him took willpower he was surprised he still had. As he dipped his head and sucked one hardened nipple into his mouth she let out a strangled sound that went straight to his cock.

Gently raking his teeth over the tightened bud, he growled in satisfaction when he felt her tight sheath clench around his fingers.

When he flicked her nipple again, he got the same reaction. Knowing it wouldn't take long to bring her to climax, he continued his assault on both breasts. Licking, laving, teasing, he didn't give her any respite as he used his tongue on her.

Her hips were bucking against him in a frantic rhythm. She was murmuring something he couldn't understand but her eyes were closed and her fingers dug tightly against his head. Using the heel of his palm he rubbed against her clit, creating more friction against the sensitive bundle of nerves.

She sucked in a deep breath and her inner walls began convulsing around his fingers. Her climax was fast and hard and the animal side of him wanted desperately to strip away his clothes and push into her. He wanted to feel that tightness pulsing around his hard length. Wanted to connect with Lyra in a way he'd dreamed about for almost two damn decades.

As her cream rushed over his fingers and her orgasm ebbed from her body, she fell almost boneless against the floor. A sense of triumph rumbled through him as he watched her. He'd put that pleasure on her face.

Her eyes opened to slits that he could just barely see in the dim room. Lyra let out a long, whooshing breath and it appeared as if she wanted to say something but couldn't find the energy.

When she tried again, he shook his head and scooped her up. Laying her on the bed, he stretched out behind her and wrapped his arm possessively around her waist. He pulled her tight against his chest. His inner wolf calmed when she didn't even attempt to struggle. Just moved into his embrace and let her head rest on the pillow. He thought he heard her murmur "thank you" but couldn't be sure.

In mere seconds her breathing and heartbeat were steady. Despite his hard-on, he was exhausted too. After killing those demons and dropping Lyra off, he'd been on the move ever since. Generally, he didn't need as much sleep as humans considering his regenerative abilities. All shifters were like that, but more so for him since he was an Alpha. Since he knew sleep might be elusive for both him and Lyra in the near future he decided to take advantage of the next couple hours. The sun would be setting soon and the moment it did, the hunt for Lyra's daughter would continue.

But if he was truly honest with himself, he stayed in the room not for sleep, but simply to hold Lyra close.

CHAPTER FIVE

*L*yra held her purse tight against her body, using it as something to ground her. Butterflies danced like mad in her stomach.

A positive pregnancy test was tucked deep inside next to her wallet. Not that she needed proof or anything. Finn would believe her. She just liked looking at it. Part of her was terrified that she was actually pregnant with a shifter's baby, but mainly she was just excited. She and Finn had been seeing each other for over six months and she knew him better than anyone. Despite her lingering worries over his possible reaction, she knew deep down that he would embrace this. It might not be something either of them had expected, but she trusted him to be supportive.

As she waited on the steps of the local library where they always met before heading out anywhere, she fidgeted with the strap of her purse. When she saw his familiar form striding up the stone steps her stomach plummeted.

Something was wrong. She could see it written in every line of his face.

Wake up! She yelled at herself to open her eyes. This dream had been haunting her for what felt like forever. Wake up, wake up. Finn's scent twined around her and she could feel the sluggishness of the dream weighing her down, taunting her.

Suddenly everything morphed, jerking the horrible memory away and shoving something else right in her face with the intensity of a stinging slap.

"Mom?" Vega's voice tickled lightly against her senses.

Then Lyra could see her face, even if it was blurry and faded, like watching a really old film. They'd had just two connections like this very recently—ever since Vega had turned sixteen—though only while sleeping. Lyra had no psychic abilities whatsoever. She was incredibly strong and fast— more so than most vampires because she was a blood-born— but the recent psychic connection was all from her daughter.

The first time her daughter had reached out to her by accident. That time Lyra had had a clear vision of her daughter, not this blurry image. As Vega was getting older her psychic powers must be growing—possibly because of her mixed heritage, they just didn't know.

Lyra clung to the remnants of sleep now, not wanting to wake up.

Reaching out psychically, she said, "Vega? Is that you?" Please don't be just a figment of my imagination.

"It's me...drugs making me out of it..."

Even though Lyra wanted to ask her daughter a hundred questions and apologize for fighting with her, she knew how fragile this moment was. How easily it could slip away from them. "Honey, where are you?"

"Dunno exact...didn't go far. Heard one say...still in Biloxi." Even Vega's voice in their dream was slurred.

Her heart jumped at that. Her daughter was nearby. "Have they hurt you?" Lyra's throat tightened at the thought of anyone harming her.

"No...guy guarding me is kinda nice...can hear the ocean," she mumbled.

Everything started to fade. The vision of her daughter's face was dissipating. Reaching out, she tried to grab onto the fuzzy image of Vega but it was useless. "I'll find you!"

Jerking upright, Lyra found herself clutching onto a pillow in the middle of Finn's giant bed. He was gone, she realized as she looked around the room. Her entire body shook and she had to fight back the tears. Her daughter was alive and unharmed. That was the most important thing. She needed to tell him Vega was in Biloxi. It was a big city but Lyra didn't care. They *would* find her.

Swallowing convulsively, she looked down at her naked body and cringed at the thought of how Finn had helped her get to sleep. One more thing she could add to her list of stupid decisions. Getting involved with him in any way right now was just plain insanity.

She slid off the bed and slightly pulled the curtain back. When she saw pink and orange streaks fading across an increasingly gray sky, she rushed to Finn's bathroom. Not bothering to look at herself in the mirror she took a quick shower then towel dried her hair. After dressing in dark pants and a dark sweater, she began tugging on her boots. As she zipped up the second one, the bedroom door flew open.

Finn looked just as big and intimidating as ever and she couldn't stop the heat that rushed to her cheeks as she remembered the way he'd very recently stroked her to orgasm.

Immediately she stood. "I spoke to Vega."

His dark eyebrows rose as he shut the door behind him. "Did her captors call again?"

"No...she came to me in a dream." Lyra knew she should be more thankful to Finn for helping her sleep, but she didn't want to even think about that.

"What did she say?"

"They haven't taken her far, she can hear the ocean—and she's still in Biloxi. She also said that whoever is guarding her is nice." Which slightly soothed Lyra's panic. If Vega wasn't being mistreated or abused, Lyra could better find the focus to track her daughter down.

He was silent for a beat then said, "One of my guy's tracked her cell to its last known location but it was just outside the hotel we already checked so it's a dead end."

Hope jumped then faded inside her so quickly she felt as if she was on a rollercoaster.

Finn continued. "But, we might have a lead. Got a call from a jaguar shifter who lives around here. Said he needed to talk to me about the missing girl, but wouldn't do it over the phone."

"Did he say her name? Did he know anything about her location? Are you sure it's even Vega he's referring to?"

His expression was grim. "All he told me was he needed to talk to me about the 'vampire chick's daughter' and that it was important."

"Where does he want to meet? And when?" If her daughter was still in Biloxi she was ready to rip the city apart, but knew that was a stupid impulse. They had be smart, move quietly, especially after that warning from one of her captors.

Finn glanced at his watch even though she was sure he knew exactly what time it was. "Now, but—"

Hands balled at her sides, she took a step toward him. "If you think you can stop me from going with you, you're out of your mind."

"Lyra—"

"Don't. This is my daughter. You can leave without me but I will follow. And if you or any of your people try to restrain me, I will rip you to shreds. I'm not some weak female who needs protecting. Vega is my daughter." Her voice was barely above a whisper and her claws had begun to dig into her palms as she tried to steady her breathing.

He scrubbed a hand over his face then shook his head sharply. "You can come, but you will be quiet the entire time. I talk to him and you listen. There's no room for emotion in this. We need to keep a level head."

She gritted her teeth and nodded. "Fine." She could be as level headed as he wanted, but if this guy knew where her daughter was, he was going to tell them. Or he'd lose his head.

"Tell me about your daughter," Finn said as he steered out of the main gates to his home. He'd wanted to ask earlier but it hadn't been the time. She'd been too distraught, but now he could see she was better focused. The psychic connection with her daughter had obviously helped. He hoped talking about Vega would help Lyra's focus even more.

"She's smart, resourceful, beautiful and...so young and vulnerable." Her voice cracked on the last word.

"What about school? How's she doing?"

Lyra glanced at him, a touch of surprise on her features. "Very well. She graduated from high school early and decided to take a year off until she figures out where she wants to go to college."

"Did she go to a regular high school?" He frowned, wondering how that was possible.

Lyra nodded, her blonde hair falling over her shoulders. She slightly tilted her face away from him, as if she was hiding her expression. "She's free to walk in the daytime because of the genetics from her father. Of course she's had to hide some of her abilities, but we've made it work. When I was… when we moved out on our own it was a conscious choice to give her the kind of childhood I never had."

Something about the tone of her voice and scent was off. "On your own…how long have you lived away from your coven?" It was one of the answers he'd been trying to find out through discreet inquiries.

She swallowed hard enough that he heard it, her face still turned away from his. "A while."

He wanted to press her for more answers but didn't want to upset her before they made it to Bo Broussard's club. It was the only neutral place Rene Bellanger—the jaguar shifter who'd contacted him—would agree to meet. Finn had decided not to point out that whether it was 'neutral' or not, he ruled all of this territory and could rip his throat out in the middle of the club with no repercussions if he saw fit.

"So what do you think about this guy we're meeting?" Lyra asked, smoothly changing the subject.

He could let the matter of her daughter and whatever she was hiding from him drop—for now. And he *knew* she was keeping something from him. He could scent subtle half-truths rolling off her when she spoke about Vega. Not that it would stop him from helping Lyra. *Nothing* could do that. "His name's Rene. He's a jaguar shifter who lives in my territory. He's always kept to himself, but he called me frantic and refused to talk about anything over the phone. He sounded terrified. It's odd that he wanted to meet in person."

"Do you think he has something to do with Vega's kidnapping?"

Finn shook his head. "I can't imagine him being involved, but..." He shrugged. He couldn't afford to rule anything out.

She was silent as she settled against the seat, but she turned her body more toward his. Crossing her legs in his direction, he watched out of the corner of his eye as her foot bounced up and down. She'd never been able to sit still when she was nervous.

"How has it been being Alpha of such a large territory?" she asked quietly, the question taking him off guard.

His hands tightened on the wheel. There was another question she didn't ask, but he heard it just the same. *Did he regret leaving her before taking over as Alpha?* He'd asked himself the same question too many times to count. But there was no simple answer. Yes, he regretted leaving her, but he didn't regret it at the same time. Not when he knew in his gut that he'd kept her safe, kept her alive and away from his uncle. "Rocky at first, but anyone who disagreed with my rules had the choice to leave the territory." They'd also had the choice to challenge him. Some had. They hadn't survived.

"Hmm."

He shot her a sideways glance.

The look in her gray-violet eyes was frosty. "I guess your pack's stance on vampire-shifter relations has changed considering you're helping me."

It wasn't formed as a question, and he knew what she was implying. Unfortunately he couldn't afford to get into any of that now. If he did, they would miss the meeting and they'd just arrived at the club. He kicked the truck into park. "We're here."

Hurt flashed across her face for a brief second before she got out of the vehicle. By the time he'd rounded the truck, her expression was completely unreadable. Now that darkness had fallen there were a lot more cars in the parking lot. Even so, with his over-sensitized hearing he still couldn't hear any music from inside the club. Bo had some serious sound proofing.

"What is this place?" Lyra asked, looking around.

"You'll see," he murmured. The same bouncer from earlier opened the door for them. This time he didn't say anything, just nodded politely.

The place was packed. Finn was surprised by the sheer number of vampires there, but after a quick scan of the place, wasn't remotely threatened by anyone. After ordering a couple drinks, they headed to the private booth he'd reserved—and Lyra had sucked hers down before they'd even reached it. He'd just bought a drink to be social but she'd ordered blood.

"You should have told me you were hungry," he snapped out, harsher than he'd intended to sound.

She snorted, the sound so inelegant it made him laugh. Lyra seemed startled by his reaction, but gave him a tentative, almost nervous smile that reminded him so much of the first time they'd met. It pierced his heart with a jarring kind of pain that stripped him bare. Some days he wished he could turn back time. Maybe if he'd made a different choice things would have turned out differently. Or maybe he'd have gotten her killed because of his selfishness.

But if things had worked out, he'd have been the one who'd fathered a child with Lyra instead of some nameless, faceless, irresponsible vampire. The chance of that kind of mating was impossibly rare, but in his fantasy world he and Lyra had a family together. At that thought, something tickled his memory bank. He tried to put his finger on it, but the thought was annoyingly elusive. He felt as if he should be remembering something, but couldn't. As he racked his brain, his cell buzzed in his jacket pocket.

It was Rene. *Be there in five minutes.* Finn relayed the message to Lyra who'd already ordered and drank half of her next drink. She almost seemed to relax at the news.

But the more minutes that ticked by, the edgier they both got. One hour, then two passed. After texting Rene a dozen times, he placed a few bills on the table and they left.

Once alone with Lyra in the parking lot, he readied himself for her rejection as he slid an arm around her shoulders. To his surprise she leaned into him and braced a hand against his chest. Leaning his chin against the top of her forehead, he was silent for a long moment.

She broke the silence, her voice shaky as she pulled back to look at him. "Finn, there's something I need to tell you—"

His phone buzzed again, breaking them apart. Her breath caught as he looked at the caller ID. He shook his head. "It's not Rene." But it was Gabriel. He'd had his Guardian run Rene's phone records before they'd even met with the guy. Normally Finn had someone else in his pack take care of stuff like this but he was playing everything close to the chest. Sure his pack knew he'd been housing a vampire, but Gabriel was the only one who knew exactly *why* she was there. He planned to keep it that way until he had a better grasp of what was going on.

Rene's phone off or dead. No way to track. Will keep trying. Also found listings of recently rented beach houses in area. Check email for addresses and advise further instructions.

After what Lyra had told him about her daughter hearing the ocean, Finn had also had Gabriel run down a comprehensive listing of recently rented beach houses in the area. Since it was winter a lot of those homes would be closed, but it still might be a big number to search. He didn't like the thought of involving anyone other than Gabriel in the search just yet. After seeing how many places there were to check, he would decide exactly who to involve. It wasn't that he didn't trust his pack, but Lyra was still a vampire and some prejudices ran deep among his kind.

"We might have a starting point," he said to Lyra as he opened the passenger door.

Her face was a mask, but her eyes sparked with too much hope for him to even think about letting her down. If he had to tear apart the entire city they'd find her daughter.

He held the door for her, but as she slid into the seat, he heard a very soft clicking sound. She heard it too. Her eyes widened and before he could move, she used her lightning fast vampire speed and lunged at him. Using her strength and agility she wrapped her arms around his waist, shoving him onto the front of the car next to his.

Rolling them, he placed his body between Lyra's and the truck as they dove over the other car. An explosion ripped through the air, the concussion of the sound vibrating through his ears, making his teeth shake.

Glass and debris rained down on them. Something sharp pierced his back and one of his legs but he kept his position. Lyra was shouting something at him but he couldn't make it out. He was pretty sure one of his eardrums had ruptured.

He blinked and shook his head as his hearing suddenly and very sharply came back. Thank God for supernatural healing.

Lyra reached up and stroked his cheek, concern in her face. She wiped at his jaw line, fury in her gaze as she drew back blood. "You could have died," she whispered, fear and more than that—raw anger—in her trembling voice.

You could have too. Before he could point that out, her eyes narrowed, the raw rage pulsing off her like a live wire. He'd never seen this side to her before. "I know this might have been a setup by that guy Rene, but is it possible someone in your pack was behind this? Exactly who knew where we'd be tonight?"

There were any number of possibilities of who was behind this kind of attack. None of them good. When he found out who'd tried to kill not only him, but Lyra, heads would roll.

CHAPTER SIX

"What are you doing?" Lyra asked, wiping the gravelly dust off her pants as she hurried after him.

"Hold on," he muttered, his phone up to his ear as he strode across the parking lot.

"What the hell happened?" Bo asked. Either he'd seen the explosion on a video feed or one of his employees had told him.

"Someone rigged my SUV to blow. You get anything on video?" Because Finn knew the half-demon had the entire place under surveillance.

"I'm scanning the videos as we speak. You guys okay?"

"We're fine. I'm leaving though. I'm sending some pack members to clean it up." Including one of his trackers to see if he could find anything Finn hadn't been able to scent. Normally he'd stick around, but he wanted Lyra far away from this. Glancing over his shoulder, some of his tension eased when he saw that no one from the club was coming to check it out. Bo was probably keeping everyone on lockdown for the time being.

"All right. I'll keep the scene secure. Humans won't be a problem," he added.

Finn already knew that though. The place was back far enough from any main roads that unless you knew where it was, no one should be in the vicinity of the warehouse. And Bo owned all the surrounding property as an extra buffer. If for some reason human law enforcement showed up, someone at the club could convince them to leave using psychic persuasion. As a rule Finn didn't like the practice, but when it came to hiding the existence of supernatural beings, he made an exception.

The second he hung up, Lyra gently touched his forearm. The feel of her fingers on his skin was electric. After all these years he shouldn't be affected by her so damn much. Looking down at her, he didn't pause. "I want you away from there."

She frowned, but kept stride with him. "I didn't scent anything other than explosive materials, but we might have missed something. We should go back."

He knew she was right. But that wasn't happening. If the explosion was part of a staged attack, it could have been the first element in a strike against him. Or more likely her. He couldn't completely rule out someone trying to take over his territory; that this had been orchestrated because a new Alpha wanted to move in. But he was ninety-nine percent sure it wasn't another Alpha.

No self-respecting shifter would resort to these tactics. It would make them appear weak. Another Alpha would just challenge him to a fight to the death.

No, his gut told him this had everything to do with Lyra's missing daughter. Glancing away from her, he shot off half a dozen texts, sending orders to his pack-mates. One to Gabriel, four to his most trusted warriors and one to his best tracker. "I'm sending a tracker in," he murmured as he read his packmates' affirmative responses.

Sliding his phone into his pants pocket as they reached a neighboring, empty warehouse, he stopped once they were behind it for privacy. No security flood-lights flipped on, but with their eyesight and the moon-light, they could see everything clearly. For a mile behind the warehouse was another gravelly area of flat land so he wasn't worried about a surprise attack. After he'd scanned the surrounding area visually and using his heightened scent, he turned to face her. "My trackers are better at hunting unique scents than you or I."

Her lips pulled into a thin line as she nodded. "I figured. I just don't like leaving the site unsecured." She peered around the corner of the warehouse in the direction of the totaled vehicle before moving behind the building once again.

"Bo is watching it and my packmates will be here in less than five minutes." Gabriel had already been on standby when Finn had told him he was coming to Bo's place. His Guardian had been pissed Finn was going alone with Lyra, but he didn't give a shit.

She crossed her arms over her chest, her expression fierce, though worry lingered in the depths of her eyes. "What now?"

"Gabriel's on his way with a new vehicle for us. While my packmates try to hunt down the scent, we're going to start hitting up addresses of newly rented vacation homes along the beach. There are a lot."

She blinked as she digested his words. "Of course. I can't believe I didn't think of that." She shook her head, her self-disgust clear.

Reaching out, he tugged on one of her hips, pulling her close. To his surprise, she leaned into him, her piercing gaze on his. "That's good, but what about unused places? If someone is trying to hide my daughter they might just use a home closed up for the winter, not rent a place."

He nodded at her reasoning, something he'd already thought of himself. The truth was, whoever had taken her daughter could even *own* a home, which would make searching that much more difficult. But he had to narrow down search zones somehow until he had a better lead. "It won't be just you and me hunting for her. My Guardian will be helping us and so will four of my warriors. The tracker will be trying to hunt down any scents from the bomb, but—"

"You told your packmates about my daughter?" She tried to step back, but he held firm.

She could have shoved him off if she'd truly wanted to, but she stilled, which told him all he needed to know. She was welcoming his touch even if she was angry. His other hand searched out her other hip. "I just texted them with orders to meet me to form a hunting party. Gabriel and I will divide the addresses when they arrive. My warriors didn't know about this meeting if that's what you're worried about."

At his words she relaxed a fraction. "So what are you telling them?"

"The truth. That an old friend needs help finding her kidnapped daughter and my pack will be providing all the services she needs. And, that no one else is privy to this information."

"You trust these warriors?" Her voice was hesitant.

He nodded. "With my life. They supported me *before* I defeated my uncle."

She swallowed hard and nodded. "Okay. If you trust them, I trust them." Placing her palms gently against his chest, her fingers dug into him for a moment.

The feel of her set him on fire. He hated the circumstances, but having Lyra this close was making his wolf crazy. Making him crazy with a hunger he just couldn't contain anymore.

She continued. "Thank you for doing this. You don't owe me anything and—"

Taking himself by surprise, he bent his head and crushed his mouth over hers. They'd have less than sixty seconds before his men arrived, but he didn't care. He didn't want her gratitude, he just wanted her. Had from the moment he'd spotted her in that bar all those years ago. Right now he also wanted to make her suffering stop. To give her just a few seconds of peace. Her hands fisted the front of his shirt, twisting it tightly as his tongue stroked hers, hungry and urgent. She met him stroke for stroke, her tongue flicking against his in a way that reminded him of raw fucking.

Her taste was addicting.

Erotic.

And everything he'd been missing for seventeen years.

Abruptly he pulled back, breathing hard and trying to will his body under control. His erection pressed painfully against his zipper and he wished they were anywhere else under any other circumstances. Not one where she was worried out of her mind for her daughter. Finding Vega, giving Lyra peace, *that* he could do. Hell, he'd tear this damn city apart to find her daughter. Yeah, because it was the right thing to do, but also because this was Lyra. He would do anything for this female. "I'm sorry," he said tightly, stepping back from her.

She looked as if she might respond, but at the sound of vehicles approaching they both paused and looked around the corner of the warehouse. "Is that your pack?"

"Yeah." Once the headlights turned off, he clearly recognized all six vehicles.

Seconds later four warriors, one tracker, and Gabriel and Victoria got out of their respective vehicles. Gabriel must have asked Victoria to follow so he'd have a mode of transportation. That wasn't a surprise. They had an interesting relationship; one the pack had speculated about, but Finn knew the truth. They were more like brother and sister than some true pack siblings. They would both die for each other, but anything sexual—hell no.

"Come on," he murmured to Lyra as they headed across the lot.

He watched out of the corner of his eye as Lyra continued scanning the area, ever vigilant. As they neared his packmates, he sensed the tension rolling off them as they eyed her. Well, from everyone but Victoria. She just watched Lyra with open curiosity but that was it. No hostility or anxiety. It was one of the reasons he liked the tall shifter. She almost never judged you unless you gave her a reason to.

Knowing there was no time to waste, he looked at his tracker Spiro first. "Someone rigged my vehicle to explode with me in it. See if you can pick up a scent on anything." He placed a light hand on Lyra's shoulder and watched as seven sets of eyes tracked the movement, but he ignored them. "Rule out her scent now. Anything else unusual, report to me immediately. Track if you can."

Nodding, Spiro moved into action, the lean shifter not questioning his order. Next he focused on the remaining warriors. "Did you all receive the list of addresses from Gabriel?"

At their nods, he continued. "This is my friend Lyra. Her fifteen-year-old daughter has been kidnapped and is being held somewhere in the city. Our objective is to rescue her. Her captors should be taken alive if possible, but dead works too." The only reason he wanted them alive was to question them. Then he would take their lives. As an Alpha, he couldn't let the kidnapping of innocent females in his region go unpunished. Even if it had been acceptable among his kind, his own moral compass would never allow it.

"At this point all we know is that we're looking for a location near the ocean. Lyra and I will take the first ten addresses." From there he ordered his four warriors to each take the next set of ten, making sure the locations they would be searching were near each other so no one was wasting time driving too far in between residences.

Finn could have told them over the phone but he wanted everyone to see his support—and possessiveness—of Lyra firsthand.

He had no clue what the future held for them, but he knew what he wanted with her. To make that happen, he had to make his feelings and loyalty toward her clear now. Even more than he wanted to show his pack, he wanted it clear to her that he had her back. That she could trust him.

Jason, one of his youngest pack members, but also incredibly strong, cleared his throat. "Why are we searching for a missing vampire?" When Finn growled low, Jason held up his hands, palms out. "I'm only asking what everyone else wants to know. This vampire shows up, it's the first we've ever heard of her and now we're helping look for her daughter—I'm just curious."

"Do you need a reason to obey your Alpha's orders?" Lyra asked, her voice dripping with ice.

Finn's inner wolf smiled, all razor sharp teeth ready to strike this pup. He liked that his female—and she would be again soon—didn't back down to anyone.

Jason straightened, his jaw tightening in annoyance. Before Finn could respond, Victoria snorted. "If you need a reason to help find a fifteen-year-old kid in trouble, then you're an asshole, Jason."

The other three warriors chuckled lightly, dispelling the growing tension. As they all started to head to their vehicles, Finn stopped them. "The parameters of this mission don't leave this group for the time being." Which meant even the mated ones wouldn't tell their significant others. Something he didn't have to specify to these hardened men.

Once everyone but Gabriel and Victoria were gone, Finn looked at Lyra. "You ready?"

"How do we know she isn't lying? Or this isn't part of some other scheme to start a war between us and vamps? You don't even know if she has a daughter." Gabriel's voice was challenging, his expression deadly.

Victoria, who had already made it halfway back to their vehicle, turned on her heel, her green eyes wide. "Gabriel, what the hell?"

"My word is good enough, that's how you know." He pinned his Guardian with a hard stare, his inner wolf daring Gabriel to question him again. For how tightly he was wound, he was walking a tightrope of control right now.

After a long moment, Gabriel lowered his gaze, though nothing about his stance or expression reflected the submissive gesture. Despite his attitude, Finn knew he wouldn't have a problem with the other wolf. They butted heads all the time, but Gabriel always supported him. Even if he didn't always agree with him.

Once Finn and Lyra were in his SUV, Finn plugged the nearest address on his list into his GPS. He was familiar enough with the city that he knew where most neighborhoods were, but he didn't want to waste time.

Lyra let out a long breath as he steered out of the parking lot. "I'm sorry for any issues I'm causing with your pack."

He shrugged. "Don't worry about it. If they don't like it they can leave or challenge me."

"I'm still sorry," she said quietly. The truth pulsed off her in a wave of tension he felt and scented. "For so long I hated you for pushing me away when I came to you."

Surprised by the statement, his entire body turned to ice. He might have known she'd harbored anger, and yes hate, toward him, but hearing the words was like a silver dagger to his chest.

"Now I think you might have been right," she continued. "Even if we'd run away together, no one would have ever accepted our relationship." There was such a stark note of sadness in her voice it just embedded the dagger even farther.

"I questioned my decision every fucking day, Lyra." And every day he buried his pain just a little bit deeper. Being separated from her had given him the edge of rage he'd needed to kill his uncle. It was like he'd lost part of himself when she'd gone. And he'd blamed his uncle, his rage simmering and growing every second of every day.

Her head whipped around, her long blonde hair cascading over her shoulder in a wave. "You did?"

Jaw tight, he nodded. "After I killed my uncle I searched for you." Hell, he'd still been searching for her right up until she showed up on his front doorstep. Now he knew why he hadn't been able to find her. She hadn't been living in any covens; she'd been in the human world.

As he pulled up to a stoplight, he glanced at her to find her watching him with an unreadable expression. Finally she turned away, looking out the window.

Her silence shredded him but he wasn't sure what he'd expected. Changing the subject, he said, "As soon as we stop at the first place I'll email you the list of address-es so you have a copy too. Maybe next time you connect with Vega she'll be able to give you a clue about the place; help us narrow it down." He prayed that was so. The constant worry lines on Lyra's face were clawing at him. More than anything, he wanted to make them go away, to give her back her daughter. Then he wanted to possess Lyra once and for all. To bind them together. The rest of the world be damned.

Her lover's voice came over the phone in a whisper, as if he was afraid of being overheard: "A group of war-riors just left the mansion."

She rolled her eyes because he couldn't see her. She was growing increasingly annoyed with his whininess. He might be fantastic in bed, but as soon as they made the rest of the money they'd been promised, she might kill him too. "So what? They're probably just hunting for more demons."

A long pause. "I don't know. They rushed out of here so quickly. And when I questioned Gregory's mate she didn't know what he was up to."

"You questioned his mate?" He was dumber than she'd originally thought.

"I made it sound casual. I'm just worried they're on to us."

No, if anyone was on to them, they'd be dead. Finn would kill them for what they'd done.

"I know the money is good, but..."

"Good? The money is *insane*." Way too much to turn down. A very powerful vampire had sent out a notice to certain purveyors that he wanted to hire someone to kidnap a young blood-born vampire in this region. It had been an easy grab and bag. Well, once they'd managed to pump the little bitch full of silver.

Because she and her lover had done different jobs for extra cash in the past, they'd been contacted for the kidnapping job. Even though it had been a risk it would be worth it. The vampire who'd hired them couldn't enter this region without drawing attention to himself. He thought he was so smart; that they wouldn't realize who this little vamp was once they'd taken her. But she knew. And she intended to capitalize on the opportunity now in her lap.

"You shouldn't have double-crossed him," her lover said, as if reading her train of thought.

Him questioning her decision was even less attractive than the whining. "We didn't." She'd just changed up their plans a bit. Instead of delivering Vega Marius to the male vamp, she'd decided to keep her until the last minute possible. The male needed Vega at the eclipse, and even though she didn't know exactly why, she wasn't stupid enough not to realize that as soon as she turned over the kid, she and her lover would be killed. Now that the kid's mother had shown up in town, she understood why her lover was worried. Because deep down, she was terrified too. But not of the male vampire.

Finn was a powerful Alpha and while she'd done a few things that might have gotten her into hot water before—if she'd been caught—kidnapping a hybrid vamp who was almost definitely Finn's daughter guaranteed she and her lover would be sorry they'd ever been born if he found out. Because he wouldn't make their deaths easy.

She couldn't know for sure they had a blood tie, but the kid looked exactly like him. The midnight black hair, the sharp cheekbones, her above average height for her age. She hadn't been positive before, but now that he'd let that vampire Lyra into the pack's mansion, Vega just had to be his daughter.

She wasn't surprised he hadn't told the pack either. The fact that he'd mated with a vamp was disgusting. But that he'd had a child?

"What should I do?" her lover whispered again, shattering her train of thought.

God, his whining was beyond grating. "Nothing. Just act normal. As soon as the sun rises, we'll switch shifts. No one knows what's going on and we've been very careful. If you can just be patient, think of the payday we'll make. We can leave this place and start a new life." One with no rules and a shitload of money that could buy them anything they wanted. If she played things right, Finn would never know she'd been involved.

"Okay. Call if you need me."

After they disconnected, she peeked in the bedroom where Vega was restrained on a bed with silver chains. The young girl was sleeping and looked a little pale, even for a vampire. She might have to get her some more blood. Her contact had warned that Vega needed to be alive and if she wasn't turned over in pristine condition then the deal was off.

Frowning, she reviewed her options. She could feed the vamp from her own vein or she could find some unsuspecting human. Though she'd rather find a human, she decided it was smarter to stay inside. That way she didn't run the risk of running into one of her packmates. If her Alpha or any of the warriors even suspected what she'd done, she'd already be dead. Of that she was sure. That didn't mean she shouldn't exercise caution right now. Moving locations might be the smartest thing. She knew just the place.

CHAPTER SEVEN

Lyra opened the sliding glass door to the upper balcony of the beach house and silently stepped out onto the porch, Finn close behind her. After breaking into the twenty-fifth house on their list—and still coming up empty—they'd heard two humans entering through the front door so now they had to escape from the second floor.

She pointed at the wooden railing and raised her eyebrows. Finn nodded in agreement.

Stepping over the railing, she balanced on the small outer ledge and measured the distance down to the sandy area. It was on an incline so it was about nine feet. Wordlessly she and Finn dropped at the same time. Their boots made a puff of sound against the sand, but it was unlikely a human would hear.

Still, she followed his lead and hurried toward the beach, using her vampiric speed to fly over the sand, barely touching it. With an almost full moon hanging brilliant above them and the crashing of waves so close, it was such an idyllic night that it irked her. She felt so dark inside that everything else should reflect her feelings. "Has anyone else checked in?" she asked once they'd made it to the beach. He'd parked along the curb of Beach Boulevard and they'd been hitting up houses on foot for the past couple hours. With their speed it would take them no time to eventually return to the SUV.

He nodded, but his frustrated expression told her all she needed to know. "No luck."

"Maybe the twenty-sixth time will be a charm," she muttered as they continued down the beach. "How many down is it?" she asked as Finn pulled out his cell phone.

He'd been using a map on his cell to measure the distance between each residence. Some of the homes had had security systems, so for those they'd just used their scenting abilities. She didn't mind letting him head up this part of the search. Her entire body was shaky enough—partially from the need to eat and partially from fear for her daughter—she didn't need to be handling anything technical now. She'd been covering her hunger from him, but knew she wouldn't be able to much longer. Before she told him she just wanted to make it through as many places as they could.

"Four down from here—"

She jerked to an abrupt halt as the wind shifted and she picked up the faint scent of roses.

Vega.

Lyra's throat tightened as she struggled to force the words out. "I scent her," she whispered, knowing she wouldn't have to explain to Finn what she meant.

DARKNESS AWAKENED | 103

His entire body went rigid as he smoothly moved into a fighting stance. "Where?"

She nodded toward the pale blue two-story home with a lot of glass doors and windows. There were no lights on and the place had a stark stillness about it. Or more likely that was just Lyra's mind going into overdrive with worry. "I scent her on the air. Roses and moonlight."

"Moonlight?"

Lyra shrugged, carefully walking across the sand, trying to hold on to that scent. "In addition to the roses she smells like the winter forest at night. It reminds me of the moon." Her voice was a scant whisper in case Vega or her captors were nearby.

Finn lightly touched her forearm. When she looked at him, he pointed to the back, then himself. Next he gestured to the front of the house, then at her. She nodded in understanding.

Soundlessly she unsheathed the single blade she'd kept secured under her thick sweater and moved into action. To the human eye she would have been almost a blur of movement as she raced around the house. Once she was sure no one, either human or supernatural, was waiting to ambush her, she made her way to the front door. At this point she didn't care if there was an alarm system. Her daughter was inside and she was going to free her.

Using her inborn strength, she pulled the doorknob off and pushed the glass and wood door open just far enough so that she could slip inside. There was a faint trace of that familiar roses scent but it was overpowered by a harsh chemical, bleach smell. And she couldn't hear anyone in the house. Not a small scuffle of movement, no labored breathing, nothing. It was like a tomb. And she couldn't feel her daughter's presence even though she swore she scented her.

As raw fear clawed at her, she crept silently down the tiled hallway, following the chemical scent. Whatever it was, her gut told her it wasn't good.

When she reached the end of the hallway, she stopped at the staircase when a slight sound caught her ears. Upstairs.

Blade in hand, she flew up the stairs, only slowing when she reached the last step. It opened into an almost loft type space with a seating area that faced two big sliding glass doors. The thick curtains had been drawn back and one of the doors was open. To the left and right of her were two more doors, both partially ajar.

When the left one opened, she tensed, pulse racing, but stopped when Finn stepped out.

"The place is clear," he murmured, disappointment plain in his voice.

"I can still smell her, but it's like someone covered it with something...astringent."

He nodded and motioned toward the room he'd just exited. "It's a variant of perfumes, fragrant room spray and I'm pretty sure bleach spray... I don't know her scent but I can smell roses in here. It's heightened."

Feeling almost numb, she stepped forward, walking past him. Sometimes abject fear from any being, whether human or supernatural, could put off a sharper scent almost impossible to cover. It could linger for weeks or months, depending on the strength of the terror.

The second Lyra stepped in the room, her stomach pitched. There was a queen-sized four-poster bed, perfectly made, and the rest of the furniture had sheets draped over it. But the scent of her daughter's fear was so potent it nearly bowled her over. It wasn't just the roses, it was raw, acidic fear.

Vega was scared and Lyra wasn't there for her. It pierced her. Her throat ached as she shoved back tears. Though she wanted to break down, she was stronger than that. And her daughter deserved better. She turned back to Finn who was impossible to read. "My senses were going haywire until I reached this room. Can you trail the scent out of here?"

Clearly angry, he shook his head. "No, but I've already texted Spiro. He might be able to pick up something we can't."

Even though she was frustrated, she was grateful for the help. "Do you think...she was moved?"

He nodded. "Yeah. Let's wait outside for him. Maybe we'll catch a trail out front."

She followed Finn out, but couldn't stop the question burning a hole inside her. "Do you think—"

"Don't," he ordered, as if he'd read her mind. "They wouldn't have moved her if they didn't still need her alive. They would have just…"

Killed her. Yeah, Lyra knew that. She was glad he didn't say the words though. Once they stepped out front, an icy blast of wind rolled over her, the chill a welcome distraction.

"You've got about half an hour until sunrise. Victoria and Gabriel are on their way here too. Victoria will take you back to the compound."

Stupid fucking sun. She'd been so damn close to finding Vega. She didn't want to stop now. "What about you?"

"Gabriel, my warriors and I aren't even close to done."

Tears burned her eyes and without thinking, she wrapped her arms around him, holding him tight. She was terrified for her daughter and without Finn she didn't know what the hell she'd be doing. Even though she was grateful for his help she couldn't find the words to tell him. She knew if she opened her mouth again, she'd have a full on melt down of tears.

Thankfully he just wrapped his arms around her and held her tight, his embrace the only thing keeping her standing against the weather of emotions raging through her.

"I like the name you chose for your daughter. Vega, the brightest star in the constellation Lyra. Very smart," Victoria said, the first words she'd spoken since they'd pulled away from the beach house.

Lyra blinked in surprise. Almost no one ever got that connection. "Ah, that's correct."

"So she's the brightest star in your world."

Lyra smiled despite the suffocating agony pressing in on her. Right now her star was missing and she would do anything to get Vega back. "Yes. From the moment she was born."

"Vega has been called the second most important star in the sky—after the sun of course," the female shifter continued.

"I'm surprised you know that."

"I know a lot," she said matter-of-factly.

"Oh."

Her green eyes widened and she shot Lyra a quick look full of concern. "I'm not being arrogant, if that's what you think. I just seem to retain random facts. A *lot* of them." Victoria cleared her throat. "I also know that before they were all wiped out, the Akkadians called Vega the Life of Heaven."

Lyra went still at the shifter's words, wondering where she was going with this. A long, tense pause seemed to stretch out forever in the SUV, but Lyra had nothing to say.

"When Gabriel told me your daughter's name it triggered an obscure memory, especially with the rise of these monstrous Akkadian demons. According to an ancient Sumerian prophecy, the Life of Heaven can open the gates of hell."

"So? Sumerians and Akkadians were two different cultures." Damn it, why was she even discussing this? She was just opening up dialogue about something she had absolutely no wish to discuss.

"Maybe so, but their language and way of life intersected on a massive scale until the Akkadian language completely replaced the Sumerian one."

"Why are you telling me this?" Lyra didn't want to play word games with this woman.

Victoria shrugged in a maddeningly casual way. "The prophecy also says the Life of Heaven is destined to open it in its sixteenth year. I know your daughter is only fifteen and usually prophecies are vague—and can be interpreted any number of ways, but…" She trailed off and looked at Lyra pointedly.

"Say whatever you need to say."

"I just find it interesting that your daughter's name is Vega and that she's been kidnapped right as Akkadian demons are already being unleashed."

Lyra was silent as she tried to formulate a response. There wasn't a correct one and she wasn't sure what this female's endgame was. If Victoria even had one. But Lyra had learned long ago never to trust anyone. "Who else knows about this prophecy?"

"I'm sure scholars of history are aware, but if you're referring to the pack, no one that I know. I wasn't kidding when I said I have a lot of random knowledge rolling around in my head."

"Have you told Finn?"

"No."

"Why not?"

A shrug. "He's already trying to find the girl. This knowledge won't help him. Besides, I'm pretty sure he already knows way more about the prophecy than I do. Just as I'm sure *you* know more about your daughter's kidnapping than you've told us. There's probably some vampire prophecy with the same sentiment."

That hit way too close to home. "You're too smart."

"Everyone tells me that."

The sky had turned a lighter gray at the edges of the horizon, but they were less than thirty seconds from the house so she was thankful Victoria stopped speaking. Right now she just wanted to be alone. Maybe if she could get some sleep she could connect with Vega again; find out where the hell she'd been moved to. What if it was out of the city? What if—

Victoria's voice cut through her thoughts. "Finn is a good Alpha. He's a good *man.* He took me in when I was a cub and didn't have anywhere to go. I don't want to see him hurt."

Lyra nodded at the abrupt change of topic, under-standing the woman's meaning. She tried to ignore the sting of it. Just because she and Finn didn't have a future didn't mean she needed to be reminded of it. She was well aware that a vampire and Alpha wolf would never work. It would be hard enough for a regular wolf and vampire to work, but an Alpha? Try impossible. "I know. As soon as I have my daughter, I'll be leaving." It might not be as simple as that because Vega would sure-ly want to spend time with her father. Of course Finn would most definitely kick Lyra out of his life once he discovered the truth. Her head ached as she thought of the fallout.

Victoria frowned as she steered through the open gates toward the mansion. "That's not what I mean. I'm twenty-three now, but I was ten when Finn took me in.

DARKNESS AWAKENED | 111

In all that time, I haven't known him to take a lover. Definitely not within the pack. He's never touched one of our females and believe me, the women have *tried*. Some of them would love nothing more than to bed our Alpha. I'm not saying he hasn't searched out companionship, but if he has, no one knows about it."

That was a surprise. A big one. Lyra didn't even know how to digest it. If it was true, it meant that she'd held a place in Finn's heart just as long as he'd had one in hers. She wanted to curse at Victoria for telling her. She didn't want to know that Finn hadn't taken up with another female. Okay, that was a huge lie.

The knowledge soothed the darkest, most possessive part of her that wanted to claw to shreds any woman who'd been with Finn after her. Now it turned out there might not have been any. But that was impossible. It had to be. She refused to believe otherwise. It had been much easier to paint him as a bastard who'd turned his back on her and never thought of her again.

"Thank you for telling me." The female hadn't needed to.

She gave her a half smile. "I figured you'd want to know."

CHAPTER EIGHT

"**M**om?" Vega sounded stronger than before.

"I'm here, honey. Are you okay?" It was a stupid question. Of course her daughter wasn't okay.

"The female moved me to a new place. She's...scared. She covers her scent with gross perfumes, but I can smell her worry."

"Do you know where she moved you? Has...anyone hurt you?" She couldn't get the scent from the bedroom out of her head. The acidic panicky fear left behind was embedded in Lyra's memory.

"No one's hurt me other than keeping me in silver chains and pumping me full of drugs."

Knowing what her daughter was going through made Lyra see red. "You sound stronger now. Are you sleeping?" Lyra could only connect with her daughter when she was asleep, but Vega was the one with the strong psychic abilities. Vega could contact her whenever she was strong enough.

"No, I'm awake. The woman's gone, but her male partner is here now. He's nice enough, but stupid. When he checked on me I pretended to be in pain so he didn't give me any more drugs. The chains hurt, but without the drugs I might be able to get out of here."

Lyra could feel the psychic link thinning and fought to hold it. Even though she was asleep she wasn't in full fighting form. She needed to feed to regain her strength. Desperately she tried to mentally grasp onto their link. "I'm working with the Stavros pack to find you. We're doing everything we can to bring you back."

"You're really working with...him?"

"Yes." No time to dwell on that. "Is there anything you can think of that might help us locate you?"

"When we were driving, I heard...like, carnival sounds. She had me blindfolded, but it sounded like a carnival. I don't know how else to describe it. It felt like we were idling at a stop sign or stoplight. After that we drove for maybe five more minutes before stopping. Afterward she pumped me full of more drugs, but they're wearing off quicker now. I think I might be building up a tolerance or something. I don't know."

"That's good, honey. Just stay strong. I will find you, I swear." Or die trying.

"I will, Mom. I miss you and I'm so sorry for the way I left—"

"Stop. I don't care. You had every right to leave."

"No, I..."

The link shattered as Lyra woke up.

Sucking in a sharp breath, she jolted up in Finn's bed. Heart pounding wildly, she looked around the dark room. A carnival. Scrambling for her phone, she snagged it from the nightstand and tried calling Finn.

When he didn't answer, she texted him what Vega had told her.

Though her internal clock already told her that the sun had set, she pulled back the curtains and opened the outer shutters to reveal the twilight sky.

After dressing and strapping on her weapons, she tried calling Finn again, but he didn't answer. Frustrated, she left his room. It wasn't as if she was a prisoner.

The long hallway that led to the stairs was empty, but she could scent shifters in some of the nearby rooms. As she descended the stairs she saw a couple talking near the entryway. When they spotted her they watched her cautiously, as if they were afraid she would attack. Though she was tempted to bare her fangs she restrained herself.

Instead she asked, "Have you seen Finn or Victoria?"

They seemed surprised she'd spoken to them, but the female motioned to the front door. "Victoria just stepped outside. I think she's going running. Finn hasn't been here all day."

Which meant he'd been hunting for Vega all day without any sleep. That knowledge warmed her from the inside out. "Thanks." Stepping past them, she strode out into the darkening night.

And froze.

At least a dozen Akkadian demons were spread out on the property, their glowing yellow eyes stark against the darkening night. With her heightened vision she spotted them attempting to use trees as cover, but the giant reptilian-skinned creatures simply couldn't hide. They stank too much anyway. The sulfuric scent had already started permeating the air.

Five wolves that she could see were fanning out. Before she could head back in to warn the others, a loud, eerie howl rent the air. Almost immediately the air was filled with answering howls. Oh yeah, that was warning enough.

Without pause she whipped out her blade and let the claws on one hand free. Behind her she could hear more shifters exiting the house, but she tuned them out. She raced down the small steps, her boots slamming against the stone walkway until she hit the grass. All around her demons and wolves clashed so she went for the closest demon.

She ran at him full speed, internally smiling when he braced for her attack. At the last second before impact, she jumped into the air, positioning herself over him. As she came back down behind him she turned in mid-air and sliced down with her blade.

It only took one sharp slice to decapitate the beast. As the arterial spray blasted outward in an arc, she jumped back to avoid it. Turning away, she saw more and more of them converging across the property. To her left and right wolves ripped and shredded at the beasts.

Triumphant howls and cries of agony filled the air. Sounded like the wolves were winning, but that could change in an instant. Who knew how many of these things there were?

Moving into action again, she raced up a tree half-flying, half-climbing, when she spotted another one trying to hide amongst the leaves. It snarled and hissed as she jumped onto the fourth branch and tried to scramble away. This one was only about five feet tall, even smaller than her.

It jumped down from the branches, but before it hit the ground, an all black wolf flew through the air, ripping its head off in one fluid bite. As the wolf's paws slammed against the grassy earth, it howled victoriously then looked up at Lyra and yipped.

She could be wrong but the green eyes looked exactly like Victoria's. Lyra jumped back down next to her. There was no time to pause before she launched herself at another demon.

It was like they were multiplying. She wasn't sure how much time passed as she sliced and clawed her way through them. Maybe half an hour, maybe longer.

After killing one of the seven foot versions, she whirled, ready for another attack, and saw only bodies of the dead demons littering the lawn. There were a few injured wolves limping back toward the main house, but she didn't see any casualties. The property was large though so she couldn't be sure.

Weapon ready, she scanned the thicket of trees. When she saw Victoria changing to human form she hurried toward her.

The tall, dark-haired female's expression was grim. "I think they're all dead."

It was a little jarring to be talking to a completely naked woman, but that was the least of her concerns now. "What the hell was that? Has that ever happened before?" Finn hadn't mentioned the demons breaching the property like that. He'd just said his pack had a problem in the city.

"That was pure insanity," Victoria muttered. "And no, that's never happened."

"Do you know why Finn isn't back yet?" She doubted he'd been hurt, but she couldn't fight the worry she had for him.

"I don't know." Victoria's head tilted to the side for a second as if listening for something. Then Lyra heard it too.

The main gate opening.

Skirting around the corpses, they hurried across the massive property until they reached the long, winding drive. Gabriel, Finn and the shifters she recognized from their earlier search were all getting out of their vehicles.

Everything else around her funneled out as she spotted Finn. His military-style fatigues were dirty, his long-sleeved shirt was ripped and the coppery scent of blood and sulfur clung to him as she hurried toward him.

Keeping her gaze locked on his, she ran her hands down his chest, needing to know he was okay. "Are you hurt?"

Something flashed in his eyes as he shook his head. "No, but what the hell happened here?"

"A shitload of demons attacked the place," a male said. "It wasn't well thought out from a strategic point of view, but they must have thought they had numbers on their side."

She turned and was surprised when Finn wrapped his arm tightly around her shoulders. In front of his entire pack. She returned his embrace as they faced everyone.

"Injuries?" Finn asked.

"Nothing major. Everyone who was here when the fighting started is accounted for," the same dark-haired male said.

Almost all the wolves were still in animal form, but a few had changed back to human. It surprised her when Gabriel shoved his shirt at Victoria. The female just rolled her eyes but put it on.

"Burn the bodies. We're on lockdown for the night. I'm going hunting tonight with Gabriel and a handful of warriors but everyone else remains here." Finn looked at the same male who had spoken twice now. The man was clearly a warrior. "Make sure no one leaves. I want a list of everyone off-property and I want you to contact them. Everyone needs to get back in the next hour."

The man nodded, then flicked a look at Lyra. "Thank you for fighting," he murmured quietly before heading back to the house.

After that, all the wolves started moving toward the home, some shifting, some remaining wolves. But everyone listened to Finn. She knew in a few minutes, the demons would all be ash.

Before she could question Finn, he turned to Victoria. "Are you strong enough to heal those injured?"

"Of course. I'll let you know if anything is serious." As Victoria strode toward the house, Lyra saw others starting to burn the demons' bodies.

"What happened to you guys?" Lyra asked, looking at Finn and the others.

"Same thing that happened here. We caught a group of them about a mile from here... I got your text." He quickly changed the subject. "The state fair is in town, it might be what she heard. Spiro used the details you gave to narrow down her possible holding area to two miles. I wanted to come back and get you."

Pumped up on adrenaline, she nodded. "I'm ready to go." She still needed to feed, but wanted to get to her daughter a lot more.

"We need to change clothes in case we run into any humans, but we'll be out of here in less than sixty seconds."

"Okay."

He dropped a quick kiss on her forehead before nodding at his men. With the exception of Gabriel and Spiro, they hurried toward the house.

Ignoring Gabriel, she looked at Spiro. "I know you're doing it for your Alpha, but thank you for trying to track my daughter."

He nodded and gave her a half-smile that was actually reflected in his eyes. "No problem. We're going to find her."

Gabriel cleared his throat, drawing her attention to him. His expression wasn't hostile—like earlier—but it was cautious. "How is it that you know she's near the ocean? Or heard the carnival sounds? If she's kidnapped, how are you in contact with her?"

They were fair questions, but until she knew who was holding her daughter, she wasn't telling anyone other than Finn anything. "Have you already asked Finn these questions?"

Jaw tight, Gabriel nodded.

And clearly Finn hadn't told his Guardian or the wolf wouldn't be asking her. "How long have you been Finn's Guardian?" she asked instead of answering. His uncle hadn't had one—had felt having one was beneath him—but clearly Finn thought highly enough of Gabriel if he'd appointed him as his second and they weren't even related by blood.

He blinked, seeming surprised by the question. "Five years."

"He considers you a friend." A very good friend. Even Lyra could see that. It was the only reason Finn hadn't physically challenged the other male outside the supernatural nightclub. Because any blatant show of disrespect to an Alpha in front of others was usually met with violence and dominance. It was just the way wolves or any supernatural beings operated. They had to.

"Yes. I would die for him." The shifter practically growled the words, the truth rolling off him in potent waves. Unlike lies, which were acidic, this was such a fresh, pure scent.

"Good. Then trust him."

"I do trust *him*." But not her. The unspoken words were clear.

She shook her head at his intentional misunderstanding. "Trust his *judgment*."

"I've seen men do stupid things over women."

"And I've seen women do even dumber things over men. Just because you might not have all the pieces to the puzzle doesn't mean—"

Spiro cleared his throat loudly, as if they couldn't hear Finn and the others exiting the house. Lyra stopped talking only because to continue was pointless. Gabriel didn't trust her. Fine. She didn't care, and even understood to some degree. The only thing that mattered was that he helped find her daughter. Or if not help, as long as he didn't hinder their searching, he was a blip on her radar.

She turned to find Finn and the others striding down the driveway. As always, everything else around her funneled out when he was near. Dressed in clean clothes, it didn't take away from his fierceness. With military style fatigues and weapons outlined under his jacket, he looked like the warrior she knew him to be. Drawn by a primitive instinct, she took a step toward him and nearly stumbled. Before anyone noticed, she caught herself.

When those ice blue eyes narrowed on her, she frowned and looked down at her clothes. She thought she'd missed getting any blood spatter on her, but maybe she needed to change too.

"When's the last time you ate?" he demanded as he came to stand in front of her.

Okay, maybe he'd noticed. "At that club."

His eyes went pure wolf for a moment. "What about before that?"

"Before I came here."

He glanced at his men and gave fast orders, telling four of them to head to various areas, but to keep their phones on them. Then he looked at Gabriel and Spiro. "You two wait. We won't be long." Not giving her a chance to argue, he grasped her hand and tugged her toward the house.

With no choice but to follow, she hurried alongside him. "I could have just fed from you in the SUV."

He grunted as they cleared the front door. "I'm not letting anyone see you feed from me."

At his words her face flamed. She hadn't even been thinking about how turned on her body naturally got when she fed from Finn. It never happened with anyone else. She wondered if her reaction would still be the same and was glad Finn was thinking clearly. If she'd climaxed in front of others while feeding it would have been embarrassing. And she wasn't doing her daughter any good if she didn't even have the strength to fight to free her.

They went down a long hallway and through the swinging door into a massive, professional grade kitchen. Made sense it was so big with all the wolves. Surprisingly the room was empty, but he kept going until they reached a pantry door. Inside was larger than her master bathroom back at home.

Without pause he turned to her and bared his neck. He could have offered his wrist. In fact, she should have just taken his wrist, but he was making himself vulnerable in a way Alphas almost never did. He was giving her the ultimate trust with this one act. His breathing was slightly erratic and the subtle spiciness of his arousal filled the enclosure.

She couldn't reject this offer—even if she didn't deserve him. Closing her eyes, she clutched on to his shoulders and sank her fangs into his neck. That spicy scent wrapped around her like a seductive embrace.

His big body jerked against hers, his arms coming around her waist as the sweet taste of his blood coated her tongue. He let out a groan and rolled his hips against her. More than once he'd told her how erotic it was when she fed from him. That definitely hadn't changed.

Unlike what fictional movies portrayed, shifter blood wasn't poison to vampires. It was like the nectar of the gods. Most supernatural blood was like that for vampires. His blood made her stronger and invigorated her faster than human blood ever could. Since he was an Alpha...She moaned against his neck as she sucked and swallowed the sweet liquid down.

Against her will, her nipples tightened and her body pulled taut as she fed from him. Something about his blood, about him, had always done this to her. After nearly two decades of drinking human blood, the taste of Finn was like a shot of adrenaline.

He was clearly affected too. It was slight, as if he was trying to contain his reaction, but each time she sucked, he let out a shudder and she felt it all the way to her core.

She tried to keep her body rigid, to retain control as she drank, but she couldn't help the hunger growing inside her. A hunger that had nothing to do with her need for blood. Rubbing her breasts against him as she fed, she savored the way he shuddered. The scent of his arousal completely enveloped her, making her light-headed. His erection pressed against her lower abdomen and it was all she could do not to wrap her legs around him and start dry humping him like a cat in heat.

But she had pride. Sort of.

Her most primal side was threatening to take over and the only thing stopping her was the knowledge that her daughter needed her. Sometimes she hated how primitive she was. *She* was in control, not her hunger. Something she hadn't had to remind herself of since she was a young girl.

Though it felt like forever, she knew maybe sixty seconds had passed. When she pulled back she felt rejuvenated and a thousand times more powerful. The strength from his blood was pure energy. Quickly, she licked the wound to start the healing process, though it was already almost closed. Unlike a human, Finn healed with impressive speed. As she looked at him, she sucked in a deep breath.

His eyes had gone pure wolf as he watched her. She could see his beast right on the surface, his need and hunger a living thing. His gaze zeroed in on her mouth. Instinctively she licked her lips and tasted a little blood she'd missed.

"Meet you outside in a minute," he said, his voice raspy and growly, more animal than man.

Not trusting her own voice, she nodded and before she'd blinked he was gone, leaving the door open in his wake. Shoving away all thoughts of the two of them naked together, she hurried from the pantry. Now that she had her strength back, everything around her came into focus with a clarity she hadn't realized she'd been missing the past couple days.

She hadn't exactly forgotten how potent his blood was, but the energy humming through her made her feel as if she could take on a hundred Akkadian demons by herself.

As Lyra strode across the tiled floor, the swinging door opened and three she-wolves walked in. They all regarded her with surprise. Immediately the tallest of them, a blonde, lean, beautiful wolf narrowed her gaze. She crossed her arms over her chest and remained standing in front of the door. The other two; a redhead and a brunette who could compete for Miss Universe and win, both stepped to the side as if they didn't want to get in the middle of anything.

She didn't have time for bullshit. Keeping her eyes pinned to the she-wolf—because averting her gaze would be a clear sign of submission to a female like this—she sidestepped the female.

The wolf moved lightning fast, remaining in front of her. "I don't care if you're fucking Finn, we'll never accept a vampire for an Alpha female."

Yeah, Lyra already knew that. She also knew that no amount of talking would get it through this female's head that she wasn't planning to make a move as head Alpha female. Once Finn knew the truth, the tiny dream of leading by his side that she'd buried impossibly deep, would completely disappear. It would never happen.

"Move," she ordered.

"No."

Moving with a vampiric speed borne of her blood line and the shot of power she'd just received from Finn, she punched right through the woman's chest and grabbed her heart. The room went deathly silent and the blonde stared at her with wide eyes, her mouth open and gasping from the raw pain that had finally caught up to her nerve endings.

This wouldn't kill her, but it would hurt like nothing else. "If you want to challenge me later, go for it. Right now I don't have time for this crap." She leaned in closer to the female, who was making gurgling, gasping sounds as she tried to remain still. Because if she pulled back, she'd lose her heart. "Next time I'll rip your heart out and make you fucking eat it," Lyra whispered before releasing her grip and pulling her hand from the woman's body. She wasn't actually as bloodthirsty as she sounded, but her most primitive side knew that if she was anything less than coldly dominant to this female, it would be like offering her head on a platter.

The she-wolf fell to the floor, moaning and crying as her body mended itself back together. Blood pooled on the floor from the healing wound so Lyra sidestepped it and grabbed a dry rag from one of the counters. Quickly wiping her hand, she stepped toward the door once again, keeping the other two females in her peripheral.

"She doesn't speak for all of us. If you're strong and fair and make Finn happy, I don't give a shit if you're a Martian," the redhead said, no fear in her gaze.

Well that was interesting. Lyra just nodded at her and the brunette before striding from the kitchen. It was time to find her daughter.

When her phone buzzed, she fished it out of her pocket. Fear was growing inside her like out of control kudzu. That vampire bitch was impossibly fast and strong. What she'd done in the kitchen—that took incredible skill.

With shaking hands she answered the phone. "Yeah?" Glancing around, she hurried out one of the side doors. The pack was busy burning the demon bodies and cleaning up the property. No one would notice her.

"She's escaped."

Her entire body went frigid. "What?" He couldn't mean what she thought.

"I don't know how, but she's gone. Her chains are broken. She must have ripped them free."

Mind working overtime, she raced back into the house, hurrying toward her room on the first floor. "Did you give her the...medicine?" When they'd switched shifts it had been time to pump the girl full of drugs again. He'd promised he'd take care of it.

A short pause. "Yes."

Her claws unsheathed as she opened her bedroom door. She'd known him long enough that she could tell when he was lying. Looked like she'd be killing this idiot after all. Instead of showing her anger and tipping her hand, she said, "Okay. We'll find her. I'll be there soon."

Once they disconnected, she grabbed her escape bag. If the girl had gotten free, she needed to leave now. She wouldn't be wasting time searching for the girl. No, she was going to kill her partner, burn down the house they'd been in, then split town with the money she'd made. It wasn't as much as she could have made, but with the girl gone, the vampire who'd hired her would be raging pissed.

Not to mention it was only a matter of time before Finn found out what she'd done. It didn't matter that she and her partner had worn masks, that little bitch might eventually recognize her through scent. She'd been careful to change up her smell, but nothing was foolproof. She had to leave while she had the chance. Even though Finn had put them all on lockdown, she'd be gone with no one the wiser.

With everyone so distracted with the recent activity, getting out unseen should be a piece of cake. And it was her only option.

CHAPTER NINE

In the back seat of the SUV next to Spiro, Lyra looked over at his small laptop screen. He was marking off the homes the other warriors and their group had already visited. They'd been working hard the past hour; parking, splitting up then searching homes with incredible speed. Now they were moving on to another area.

After the attack on Finn's property, he was even more determined to find Vega. Lyra wasn't sure why the demons had targeted his pack, but it hadn't been a random choice. That much was clear.

"Did you see that?" Finn murmured from the front passenger seat.

"Yeah." Gabriel slowed the vehicle.

Both she and Spiro looked up. Scanning the quiet neighborhood, she didn't see anything except cars parked in driveways and a few streetlights. "What?"

"Four vampires," Finn said. "Headed down that street. Moving with purpose. Gabriel, text the other team," he ordered. Before any of them could respond, Finn opened his door and jumped from the moving vehicle. They were only going fifteen miles per hour, but his action still surprised her. Seconds later Finn jumped a nearby fence into someone's backyard, disappearing from sight.

"What are we doing?" she asked Gabriel. She knew Finn was more than capable of taking care of himself, but she didn't like him going off alone without backup.

"I'm going to park and we're following after him."

Immediately Gabriel parked next to a giant oak tree. After he sent off a brief text, presumably to the other group of warriors out searching for Vega, the three of them moved silently from the vehicle. Lyra didn't need instructions from anyone to know what they were doing. Backing up Finn and figuring out why four vamps were in this neighborhood. It was in the zone Spiro had mapped out so for all she knew they were involved with Vega's kidnapping.

Lyra used her gift of flight and took to the air. With Finn's blood flowing through her, she barely felt the effect on her energy. It was harder to track Finn's scent this way, but it was so faint anyway, she wondered if he was masking it. A gift some Alphas possessed.

When she flew over a house with an Olympic sized pool she spotted Finn facing off with four vampires. No one had weapons drawn so that was one positive point, but a familiar protectiveness rushed up inside her. She unsheathed her blade. Whisper quiet, she descended until her boots hit the grassy ground next to Finn. He didn't even flinch so she guessed he'd been aware of her presence.

The others moved back a fraction, but almost instantly the tallest of the four held up a hand to the others, staying them.

She nodded once at the male, recognizing him immediately. Justus, one of her brother's most valuable warriors.

His brown eyes widened incredulously and the tart scent that spiked off him was true surprise. "Lyra?"

The male was more like a mercenary and almost as old as Claudius. Not a blood-born, but he was over nine hundred years old. It was hard to feign the kind of surprise she sensed from him, but she wasn't stupid enough to underestimate him. "Justus."

"You know him?" Finn's voice was deceptively quiet, as if he wasn't concerned. But she knew him better than that. The quieter he got, the more focused and deadly he was.

"He's part of Claudius's coven." She didn't take her gaze off the four vamps. Behind her she heard a slight rustle of movement and tensed until she scented Finn's packmates. The backup shifters Gabriel had texted had arrived.

"Darren, Bruno, this is Lyra Marius." At that, all four of the vamps knelt briefly in a show of respect for her royal status. Though Justus hadn't introduced the third vamp, she recognized him as Christian. He was about five hundred years old if she remembered correctly.

She was confused by their action. "Why are you all bowing? And why are you here?"

As they rose, he motioned for the others to move back, a clear sign of respect to Finn. Something she appreciated. Right now the situation could turn incendiary in a millisecond.

"You're with the Alpha?" Justus asked, ignoring her questions.

"Yes. Now answer my question."

He shot Christian a quick glance, then looked between her and Finn. "I believe we might have been given misinformation. We were told you were dead and your child had been kidnapped. Claudius rescued her, but—"

"*Claudius* has my daughter?" she shouted, then remembered the humans in so many nearby homes. Panic hummed through her, raw and wild as she tried to contain her rage from breaking free. She needed answers.

"Yes." He flicked a glance at Finn, his jaw tight. "We were told two wolves had killed you, taken her and the Alpha of this region refused to punish them. Claudius rescued her, but only one wolf was there when he did. He wanted us to wait for the other one and eliminate both of them at the same time."

None of that mattered to her right now. "Where's my daughter?"

He started to answer when two of the vampires made a break for it. Before she could move, Finn and Gabriel sprung into action, their speed a little terrifying. Her hair blew back as they flew past her, pinning the two vamps to the ground. Finn gripped one of the vamps' throats, his claws slicing deep through the male's skin. Gabriel did the same to the other. The two vamps gasped and struggled, but without the ability to speak, the sounds were muted.

Justus didn't attempt to stop them, just looked at her with concern. "Something tells me you didn't leave our coven voluntarily years ago."

Now it was her turn to be stunned. "Is *that* what Claudius told everyone?"

He and Christian both nodded.

"I did *not* leave voluntarily. I was kicked out half an hour before sunrise." Her voice vibrated with anger. She had a ton of questions but only one mattered. "Now *where* is my daughter?" Humans nearby or not, she was about to lose control.

"Claudius said he was taking her back to our coven, but I don't think that's true now." He shot a glance at the two vampires who'd tried to run for unknown reasons. When he looked back at her his eyes had gone pure amber, the anger emanating off him a reminder of the type of power he possessed. Justus was not the forgiving type.

He respected power, but wouldn't tolerate a coven leader who lied.

A flood light flicked on next door and a dog barked as it raced into the nearby yard. A high wooden fence separated the houses, but they needed to find privacy. Fast.

"Where were you headed?" she asked quietly.

"I think I know," Spiro said just as low, walking up beside her.

She glanced over her shoulder to find only one other shifter. She frowned. Where were the others? She knew she'd scented them all before.

"Everyone head to the house now. I'm going to get some fucking answers," Finn growled, ripping the vamp off the ground.

She wasn't sure what house he was referring to but it was clear the others did because they all moved into action. She didn't care where it was; if it led her to her daughter, she'd go anywhere.

Finn didn't know what the fuck was going on, but he wanted answers. Being exposed with so many unsuspecting humans nearby was one of the only things keeping him restrained.

He let Lyra enter the two-story home ahead of him. Gabriel had informed him that his warriors were already waiting inside. There'd been more his Guardian had wanted to say, but hadn't. Finn had a feeling he was about to find out why.

As he and Gabriel dragged the two whimpering vamps into a living room he found Blaine and Dawn, two of his packmates cowering on one of the couches while three of his warriors guarded them.

"I remember you from the kitchen," Lyra growled at Dawn. "You were with the redhead and blonde. If you're involved with my daughter's kidnapping, what I did to blondie will be *nothing* compared to how you'll suffer."

Finn knew there was more behind that statement, but didn't ask. He scented roses. Lurking under everything else in the room, it was there. Stronger this time. Lyra scented it too. He could see the hope and fear flare in her eyes almost simultaneously. He didn't blame her after what Justus had said about her brother.

"You two," he said to Dawn and Blaine. "What the hell are you doing here? Are you involved with her daughter's kidnapping?"

Dawn started crying. The pretty brunette wrapped her arms around herself, shaking. "Blaine made me do it. He said no one would find out and no one would get hurt. It would just be easy money." Her voice shook as she averted her gaze from him, looking at her lap.

"Liar!" Blaine shouted, fear and a healthy dose of truth rolling off him.

Finn thrust the vamp he was holding at Justus. He might not know why the guy had tried to run, but innocent people didn't flee like that. First, he had another problem to take care of. Then maybe all this shit would get ironed out.

The vampire took over without question, wrapping his fingers around the whimpering vamp's neck. Finn stalked toward the couch, shoving the coffee table out of the way before he bent down in front of them. "Dawn," he growled low in his throat, letting his wolf show in his eyes.

She blinked at him, sniffling. As if she thought he'd believe her act.

"I know what kind of wolf you are. You would never let a male talk you into anything." No, she preferred to be with betas she could dominate. "Tell me the truth and I'll make your death easy. Lie and I'll give you to Vega's mother…or these vamps."

His words elicited the fear he'd hoped. Vampires could torture for decades.

She swallowed hard, but when she spoke, her voice didn't shake and all trace of tears dried up. "I have a friend that sometimes throws me odd jobs. He contacted me because a powerful vamp wanted a quick grab and bag job. It was supposed to be simple."

"Then you got greedy," Blaine spat.

Dawn lunged at Blaine, but one of Finn's warriors immediately pushed her back against the couch with ease.

Finn waited, keeping his wolf in check until he had answers. The safety of Lyra's daughter depended on it. "Continue." A deadly order.

"I knew he needed her alive. He wouldn't tell us *why* he wanted her, but it had to be for something really important because he was willing to pay us a ton of money. So..." She glared at Blaine before looking back at Finn. Immediately she dropped her gaze. "I demanded more. I knew he needed her by the eclipse in a few days."

"Do you know why?"

She shook her head and he didn't scent any lies rolling off her. But she was hard to read. One of the few wolves under his purview who was that way. He'd thought it was one of her natural abilities, but now he guessed she was just a sociopath. She'd only been with the pack less than a year and the reason he'd let her join was because so many of his warriors had requested it. All because of a pretty face. Stupid mistake he wouldn't be making again.

"Do you know where she is now?"

"She escaped," Blaine said when Dawn didn't answer.

"Is that true?"

"I wasn't here when it happened." Her voice had a bite to it.

He leaned closer. "Where is she?"

Her gaze strayed behind him, probably to the waiting vampires. "I don't know, but I don't think she escaped." She shot Blaine a disgusted look and rolled her eyes before turning back to Finn. "There's no way she pried those silver chains free by herself."

So maybe Lyra's brother did have Vega. *Shit.* "Why did you try to kill me?" Finn asked.

She blinked, true confusion spiking off her. "What?"

"The car bomb," Gabriel growled, his first words since they'd arrived. He'd never liked Dawn and now Finn realized he should have listened to his own instinct and that of his Guardian's about allowing her to join their pack.

She shook her head adamantly. "We didn't try to kill you. I just wanted to make money and we have no reason to want you dead."

Blaine looked just as confused as Dawn.

"What about Rene Ballanger?"

Blaine's expression remained blank, but Dawn swallowed hard.

"Dawn," he growled when she didn't respond.

She shrugged jerkily. "I guess he saw me and Blaine taking the girl from the hotel. He confronted me about it and tried to blackmail me into having sex with him so he wouldn't tell you." The truth was in her scent.

"You refused him?" Then likely killed him.

She nodded, her expression turning hard. "That kill was justified. Stupid asshole thought he could force me into fucking him."

Finn bit back a sigh and stood. He was as positive as he could be that she was telling the truth about everything. He looked at two of his warriors and nodded once. They understood and hauled the two wolves up. They would await sentencing back at the compound. Under normal circumstances he'd take care of them immediately, but he didn't have the luxury of time. Two of his wolves had worked with a vampire to kidnap an innocent girl and all for money. He knew what their sentences would be.

"I'm sorry, Finn! Please, I don't want to die," Blaine shouted as he fruitlessly struggled against Jason's iron grip.

"Come on," the warrior muttered, dragging Blaine off.

"I didn't know Dawn killed Rene and I never would have agreed to her scheme if I would have known the girl is your daughter. You've got to believe me!"

"Shut up, you fucking idiot," Dawn snarled.

Finn froze as the male's words registered. *His* daughter? No. Fucking. Way. Turning, he met Lyra's fearful gaze.

And saw the truth written all over her beautiful, traitorous face.

CHAPTER TEN

Lyra forced her gaze away from Finn, unable to take his accusing stare. She desperately wanted to explain things to him, especially since she realized she'd never stopped loving him. She'd been fighting the truth because it didn't matter. They didn't have a chance in hell of making things work. It also didn't matter if she deserved his wrath right now. She didn't have time to drown in guilt. Once Vega was safe, Lyra would deal with Finn.

She turned to the vampire Justus was holding. "Let him talk," she ordered.

Immediately the warrior vamp loosened his vise-like grip, but didn't let the male fall to the ground. The bloodied, now-captive vampire made a gurgling sound, his eyes bright amber as he stared at Lyra in fear.

"Can you talk?" she asked quietly, her voice as deadly as a blade.

"Yes." It came out raspy, but well enough for her to understand.

Her blood was up, roaring through her veins. "Good. Where did Claudius take my daughter?"

"Fuck you," he spat, his eyes going even brighter.

146 | KATIE REUS

Before she could say anything else, Justus withdrew a blade from behind his back and decapitated the vampire in one smooth slice.

She stepped back out of the way to avoid arterial spray as the vamp fell. Before he'd even hit the floor, he turned to ash.

Justus turned to where Gabriel held the other vampire. "Bruno, you are in front of royalty right now. You will answer her questions or your death won't be so easy." He pointed to the dust splattered against the wood floor. "I'm still torturing vampires who dared defy Claudius—thirty years ago."

Lyra wondered if that was true, but by the terror oozing off the vamp named Bruno, she guessed it was probable.

Gabriel loosened his hold on the vamp and he coughed as his neck and throat began mending itself back together. "New Orleans."

That was barely an hour and a half away. She could make that before sunrise easily. "Exact location." Her voice was a low growl as she let all her power and anger flow through her.

Bruno flicked a glance at Justus then her. "He's not going to kill her," he rasped out.

"You can't believe that," she said. She knew her brother. Besides, once he'd opened a hell gate with Vega's blood, he would want to get rid of her.

"He's not! He needs her blood to control the Akkadians once they're free."

"He thinks she's part of Kush's prophecy?" Justus demanded, as he clearly started putting the pieces together.

Bruno nodded as Finn came to stand next to Lyra.

"So he's been letting them out?" Finn asked in that deceptively quiet voice.

Lyra forced herself not to look up at him. She was doing her damndest to ignore the man, but it was impossible. He deserved answers, and once they freed Vega, she'd deal with everything he had to throw at her.

The vamp nodded. "Yes."

"Why are they in Biloxi?" he continued.

"Sent here..." He coughed once, but his neck was almost healed on the outside. "As a testing ground. Wanted to see how your pack faired against them."

"The car bomb?"

An oily scented spike of fear filled the room, making Lyra sick. The vamp didn't answer, but his fear was enough confirmation. He might have even rigged it himself, which would explain his abject terror.

"Why didn't you come to me about Claudius's plans?" Justus asked, a mixture of anger and confusion in the harsh question.

Bruno turned burning amber eyes on the warrior. "Because I agree with what he's doing! We shouldn't have to hide from these stupid fucking humans. They're dinner."

Lyra tightened her jaw so she wouldn't say something she'd regret. She'd made a good home in the human world. Humans screwed up a lot, but they also had such a capacity for love that it sometimes amazed her. Someone like him would never understand that though. And she still needed the location of her daughter so she kept her mouth shut. Right now the vamp was talking and they needed him to continue.

"The demons will destroy the planet. There won't be any humans left to rule," Justus said quietly.

Bruno shook his head, defiant. "Claudius isn't stupid. He's freeing some of them, not all of them. He wants to let them feed on the humans until they're terrified to leave their homes. Then we're going to save them."

"Vampires?"

"Yes. We'll send the demons back where they belong." It sounded like he was repeating a rehearsed speech. Or more likely Claudius had brainwashed him with it.

Lyra hadn't forgotten how much her brother hated humans—or anyone who wasn't a vampire. It wasn't a stretch to believe her brother was behind this. "And you think what? That the humans will be so happy about it they'll welcome subservience to vampires?" she asked, unable to keep the incredulousness out of her voice.

Humans might be physically weaker as a whole, but they had numbers, ingenuity and would never accept that they weren't highest on the ecological pecking order.

"It doesn't matter what they want. It's happening. And it's a good plan. One he's been working on for years. If your daughter hadn't run away from you we would have bagged her at your place. Oh yes, we've known where you were for the past couple weeks." Disdain dripped from his every word.

Lyra masked her surprise. She'd been careful about keeping her whereabouts private from anyone from her past life. Her daughter didn't have any social media accounts either. They were both so cautious, Lyra had no idea how he'd found them.

"When she ran from you, it screwed up his plans. Claudius had to hire shifters to take her." He sounded disgusted by the very thought.

Before Lyra could respond, Finn moved lightning fast, ripping the vamp from Gabriel's hand. He threw him against the nearest wall so hard a crack split right up the middle of it. Before the vamp had moved, Finn was in front of him, pinning him up against the cracked plaster. Bits of it dusted his shoulders and hair. "Give us the exact location or you'll be begging for Justus's form of punishment rather than mine."

Lyra heard none of the man in his voice, only the wolf, and though she couldn't see Finn's face, the vampire must have believed him because he started shaking. He whispered something so low even Lyra couldn't hear.

Finn dropped him then looked at one of his remaining warriors. "Keep him alive in case he's lying." Then he pinned his gaze on Lyra, so many emotions—anger and hurt being the most prevalent—in his ice blue eyes that she nearly crumbled under the intensity of it.

But she stood her ground. She might have made the wrong choice by not telling him the truth a couple days ago, but she couldn't second guess herself now. Couldn't worry about the fallout. Vega was all that mattered. "He told you the location?"

He nodded then turned toward Gabriel. "Contact Victoria and a team you trust. They need to leave immediately. We'll meet them in New Orleans."

Without a word, Gabriel moved into action, the remaining warrior dragging the vamp with him.

Neither Justus nor Christian made an attempt to stop them. As they left, Justus looked at Lyra. "We want to help you stop Claudius and find your daughter. If he truly believes she's the one to fulfill Kush's prophecy we don't have much time. There's an eclipse in a day and a half."

Lyra knew that very well. Each second that passed, it was harder and harder to control her panic. "I know." She gave him her cell phone number and was surprised when Finn did the same.

As the two vamps programmed the numbers into their phones, Finn grasped her upper arm in an unforgiving grip. Did he think she'd actually try to leave? While his hold didn't hurt, she wouldn't be able to pull away from him without a struggle. Justus and Christian both noticed and went for their blades.

She held up a hand. She'd forgotten what it was like to be considered royalty. Well, not *considered*, she technically still was. She'd just assumed her entire coven loathed her. "I'm riding over with Finn?" she said, phrasing it as a question as she looked up at him.

Jaw tight, he nodded. "You're not leaving my side." The air around him seethed with pent up emotion.

Oh yeah, he'd have a ton of questions. Some of which she wasn't sure she was ready to answer. But he deserved to know the truth. He was also insanely angry. Something she tried to ignore.

Justus nodded at Finn. "I'll try to contact Claudius. Perhaps if he believes we support his cause we can get close to him."

"You can be involved, but nothing gets in the way of rescuing my daughter. I'm leading this group. We head out now. My pack will be minutes behind us. Once we're there, my pack and I will assess the location. Claudius *will* die, but Vega's safety is the most important thing. If that means letting him temporarily escape, so be it. If you put my daughter in danger, I'll end you."

It jarred Lyra to hear Finn say 'my daughter'. Justus looked to Lyra and it took a moment for her to realize he was waiting for her approval.

She nodded. "From this point forward, we'll do everything Finn says. Vega's safety is the only thing that matters."

"And you two will ride with us. I want to hear your conversation when you call Claudius." There was no room for argument in Finn's voice and Lyra had been thinking the same thing. She was glad he voiced it.

These two vamps might be treating her with respect, but she wouldn't take anything at face value. Not with Vega's life hanging in the balance. The only thing that eased some of her worry was the fact that Claudius needed Vega alive. Her blood had to be fresh. And Lyra was determined that not one precious drop would be shed.

CHAPTER ELEVEN

Finn didn't like having anyone at his back, especially not two vampires he didn't know. So he'd ordered one of Lyra's former coven members to drive. The other vamp, Christian, was in the front passenger seat directly in front of him.

"I should have told you a couple days ago. I'm sorry," Lyra whispered, though he knew it wasn't because she was trying to keep their conversation a secret. The vamps in the front would hear everything in this enclosed space.

Finn's hands balled into fists as he tried to contain his inner wolf. Did she think that lame-ass apology was going to cut it? He couldn't ever remember being so angry. And he rarely needed to fight his beast for dominance. Right now he was walking a razor's edge of control. The wolf was right there, ready to take over. He couldn't believe he had a daughter. He hadn't even suspected Vega might be his. That kind of hybrid mating seemed impossible. "Days ago? Try seventeen fucking years ago."

She whirled on him, no longer avoiding his gaze—and apparently not caring about their audience. "I won't apologize for not telling you then! I was ready to tell you

153

that evening at the library—had already told my brother about it! Which was a big mistake in hindsight." She laughed bitterly, the sound taking on a hysterical edge. "Then *you* made the decision for us, for *me*—that it was too damn dangerous for us to be together. You just kicked me out of your life."

"It *was* too dangerous!" He didn't give a shit about their audience at that point either.

Her eyes shot sparks at him. "If it was so damn dangerous, what would the knowledge of a child have changed?" she challenged.

"I had a right to know!"

"No, you didn't. You can't have it both ways. If it was too dangerous for us to be together, then it would have been even more so for a child of ours. If your uncle would have found out about her…" She trailed off, some of the edge of her anger seeming to fade as she acknowledged the truth of how impossible their relationship had been back then.

Damn her, she was right. If his uncle had discovered Vega's existence, he wouldn't have rested until they were all dead. "You still should have told me. If not seventeen years ago, then when you first came to the compound."

"Are you freaking kidding me? I hadn't talked to you in all this time. I was terrified you'd either not believe me and then I'd still be back at square one: alone with no one to help me in the search for Vega. Or, you could

have believed me, then still kicked me out of your life—
again—and not let me help in the search. I couldn't ask
any of my human friends for help." She snorted at that,
but continued. "I had no one else to turn to and I wasn't
taking a risk you'd keep me in the dark. Finding Vega
was and *is* all that matters to me."

Finn wanted to be angry, tried desperately to hold
onto that rage, but he tried to see things from her per-
spective. Still... "I never would have kept you from finding your—our—daughter." And it pierced him soul deep
she actually thought that.

She looked away then, but not in submission. Staring
out the window at the passing cars on I-10, he could see
how tense she was. "After a couple days, I realized that. I
just didn't know how to tell you."

Scrubbing a hand over his face, he let his head fall
back. Fuck. He had a daughter he'd never known about.
With the woman he'd once loved. Had *never* stopped
loving. He wondered if Lyra knew. Hell, how could she
not? He hadn't thought twice about helping her after so
long. He'd brought her right into his pack and would kill
anyone who dared harm her.

"You went back to Claudius after I ended things?" he
asked even though he knew the answer. After what
she'd said to Justus back at the rental house it was clear
she had.

"Yeah. I swallowed my pride and asked him for shelter until I could move out."

"He kicked you out, even knowing you were pregnant?"

"*Because* I was pregnant," she muttered. "He'd apparently known about us, but hadn't cared. But when I told him... it was too much for him."

"Why not go to Titus or another coven?" He didn't know much about her other brother. Only that recently he'd had issues with a werewolf pack Finn was on very good terms with. But damn, he hated thinking of what she'd gone through alone. Kicked out of her coven with no one to help her, cut off from him, then dealing with the pregnancy, birth and raising a child all on her own.

She laughed again, that bitter sound slicing right through him. "He's worse than Claudius. They hate your kind."

"It's true," Christian murmured quietly from the front, the first words Finn had heard from the tall, lean vampire. "Claudius has archaic ideals and Titus is slowly losing members of his coven because he has the same attitude. One of his best warriors recently mated with a powerful Alpha. Times are changing and their attitudes do *not* reflect the majority of how our coven feels."

Yeah, he knew about the recent vampire-shifter mating. Rumors about it had made its way across the supernatural grapevine, but he'd heard it directly from the Alpha.

Lyra turned back from the window, but didn't respond to Christian. It was clear she was surprised though.

Finn wasn't done discussing Vega with Lyra, but he needed a mental break. Something else to focus on. Gabriel had already texted him that he and a team of warriors were on their way to New Orleans. They were likely only minutes behind them. He tore his gaze from Lyra and looked at the vamp in the front seat. "You disagree with your leader yet you followed his orders to kill two shifters you didn't know?"

"I disagree with his ideals, but he's still my coven leader. Or...he was. And I had no reason to believe he'd lied. He's always been truthful with us. Killing those who kidnapped a member of our royal line was a just order."

Justus nodded in agreement, but remained silent.

"Do you have a picture of Vega?" Finn asked after a few minutes of silence. He wasn't sure what he felt right now, aside from anger and loss that he'd been deprived of knowing his own child for all this time, but he wanted to see what his daughter looked like. Especially if... No. Hell, no. They would rescue her.

Guilt flashed through Lyra's expression for a moment as she nodded and pulled out her phone. He'd asked her if she had a photo earlier but only because he wanted to give it to the others while they were searching. She'd said she didn't have one on her.

After pressing in her security code, she tapped the camera icon then handed it to him. "I'm not much for these things, but Vega..." Tears filled her eyes as she looked away again. "She got me hooked. They're almost all of her."

He opened the first picture...and forgot to breathe. A tall, young woman with midnight black hair stood next to two other teenagers around the same age. They all wore jeans and T-shirts and had their arms around each other as they smiled widely. He didn't need Lyra to tell him Vega was his. He could see himself reflected in the young, vibrant and beautiful woman she clearly was. It was in her Mediterranean coloring, her facial structure, and that hair.

The next picture was of Vega and Lyra. Their daughter was wearing a cap and gown and Lyra wore a simple black dress. Their arms were wrapped around each other tightly. Lyra looked more like an older sister than mother in physical features, but the maternal pride she felt shined so clearly someone would have to be blind to miss it.

"She looks like you," he murmured, his chest painfully tight.

He heard her shift in her seat. "She got my eyes, but that's it. She's all you."

"She's both of us." And he didn't know how that made him feel. Overwhelmed. Proud. Awed.

She sniffled as she looked at the picture. "That was her high school graduation. It was supposed to be at noon, but after some…mental persuasion I convinced the principal it would be better to do an evening one. I wasn't missing her graduation because of a little sun."

Despite the situation, he barked out a laugh. That sounded exactly like Lyra.

"The kids loved it," she continued. "They were the first class at their school to ever have one at night. I miss her so much." Her voice cracked and when she went to turn away again, he couldn't help himself. No matter how angry he was, he could understand why she'd done what she had, and hurt like hell that he hadn't been there for her. For either of them.

He wrapped his arms around her shoulders and pulled her in tight. To his surprise, she didn't fight him, but buried her face in his neck. She didn't sob or make any outward sounds, but he felt the wetness of her tears as she slightly shook. He rubbed a hand up and down her spine. Holding her soothed the darkest, angriest part of him. If he'd been in her position, he had no idea what he'd have done.

"We'll get her back, I promise." Because any other option was unacceptable.

"I have another confession," she whispered.

He closed his eyes, not sure he wanted to hear it. Wasn't sure he could take it. "What is it?"

"She wasn't on her way to a concert. She ran away because she wanted to meet you. It's why she was in Biloxi."

Unable to speak, he tightened his grip on Lyra as he rested his chin on top of her head. His daughter had wanted to know him. Knowing that eased him a little. He was still angry, but right now they needed to support each other while they searched for Vega. Anything else would be destructive.

Vega shifted against the cold floor, the chains on her arms and legs jangling against her stone cell. She was trapped in the worst vampire cliché ever. Her crazy racist uncle had kidnapped her from her captors instead of rescuing her. Then he'd drained a pint of her blood and locked her in a dungeon of some sort. There were two other barred-in cells, one on either side of her. Both empty. At least he hadn't drugged her. Which was good and bad because now she was perfectly aware of her surroundings.

The maniac wanted to use her blood to free a bunch of hungry demons from hell in his grand attempt to take over the world—specifically humans. Seriously? What a freaking moron. Her mom had never lied about how bad her relatives were, but Vega had always thought they couldn't truly be so awful.

Turned out her uncle was way worse than she'd imagined.

At the sound of keys jangling, Vega tensed. There wasn't anywhere to go and there was no sense pretending to be asleep. She was too amped up on adrenaline.

A second later the main door beyond the three cells opened and Claudius stepped inside, his shoes clicking over the stone floor. The blond vamp was dressed impeccably in a dark suit that probably cost more than her mother made in a year. Vega could see the family resemblance, but unlike her mother, Claudius was tall and had dark brown eyes.

Dead freaking eyes.

She watched him carefully. Even though her first inclination was to verbally lash out at him, she knew that would be a stupid mistake. On the way here—wherever exactly she was—she'd seen her uncle kill one of his own vampires simply because he'd asked a question.

The guy was seriously unhinged. She wondered if it was because of his age. Her mom had told her that her parents—Vega's grandparents—had opted to put themselves in what was considered vampire stasis because they'd started turning paranoid. Later Claudius had told everyone something had gone wrong with the process because they'd died. Her mom had always wondered if he'd killed them. Something told Vega this nutjob definitely had.

Claudius stepped up to the bars of her cell and watched her for a long moment with those creepy, hollow eyes. "You're different from your mother. Not so bloody weak." He seemed pleased with that.

Vega bit her anger back. Her mother wasn't weak. She was the strongest person Vega knew. Lyra Marius had been kicked out of the only life she'd ever known with no skills and limited experience in the human world, yet had created an amazing life for the two of them. She now ran two bookstores and didn't let her aversion to daylight stop her from being successful. Vega knew her mom had needed to steal when she first set out on her own—pregnant and alone—but she'd eventually repaid all those she'd taken from once she got on her feet.

"Nothing to say?" he asked as he opened the cell door. It creaked ominously before he knelt in front of her, his expression a sneering mask of disdain.

She refused to feed his insanity, but she also wouldn't cower in front of him.

Frowning when she didn't respond, he stood and barked out an order. A moment later another vampire appeared in the main doorway. This one couldn't be much older than Vega. Maybe a decade. She could sense how young he was. Her mom had shown her how to do that. This vamp didn't exude much power. Unlike her uncle, unfortunately. That monster was coated in a thick aura of raw, evil energy.

All Vega could hope to do was escape. She wasn't stupid enough to think she could take him on all by herself. She was only sixteen and not even close to coming in to her full powers. And her uncle was over one thousand years old. No contest who'd be the victor.

Holding a syringe attached to a plastic IV bag, the other vamp scampered in, keeping his gaze locked on the floor.

"Don't just stand there, drain her," Claudius snapped.

Panic slammed into her, but she still didn't respond. Even if he could scent her fear, she wasn't going to outwardly show it. She wouldn't give him the pleasure.

The other vampire moved into action and bent down next to her. Without looking at her, he took her arm and examined her veins. "How much should I take?" he asked as he slid the needle into her vein. At least he didn't miss this time.

Last time he kept jabbing her skin because he'd been shaking so bad from fear of Claudius. Luckily she healed fast, but she didn't like getting poked with a needle. It pissed off her inner wolf. Not to mention she hadn't been allowed to run free in days so her wolf was downright agitated.

"Another pint," Claudius said, his gaze on hers, arrogant and condescending.

Good Lord, she'd never realized how great she'd had it in the human world. If she'd grown up in a coven with this guy as a ruler...ugh. Yeah, she so would have run away. Gritting her teeth, she forced herself not to speak. Calling him a douchebag would likely only incite him to take three pints. If she'd been human, she'd be dead, but with her combined shifter and vampiric healing abilities, she was only weakened.

Too weak to shift just yet. Damn him.

She looked at the plastic bag as it slowly filled with her blood and forced herself to breathe normally. No matter what, she had to reserve her strength. Once she was alone again, she'd try to think of a way out of here.

A commotion from somewhere past the main dungeon door stole her attention. She could hear multiple males shouting, then an angry roar. Definitely not a human sound. Not shifter either. Or, not wolf shifter. Of that she was certain. "Do you have a freaking bear out there?" she asked before she could remember to censor herself.

Claudius ignored her and strode from the group of cells, leaving the main door open.

"You like hurting someone unable to defend themselves?" she snapped to the vamp drawing her blood.

He met her gaze, the spike of fear rolling off him so potent, it made her nauseous. He glanced over his shoulder then looked back at her. "I don't have a choice," he whispered.

"We always have choices." Something her mom had taught her. Even if you made the wrong choice, it was cowardly to hide behind your situation. Make a decision and own it. Clearly this guy was going to be no use. Vega had thought she might be able to play up the sympathy card, but the vamp was just too scared of Claudius.

Ignoring him, she turned to the entrance as her uncle strode in with his hand wrapped around the neck of...something.

The gigantic man or animal was covered in soot and kind of an odd shape. Oh crap, he was mid shift. But what kind of animal was he? She couldn't even tell. He was a huge, dirty and lumpy figure.

Claudius threw him into the cell next to hers. The being howled in rage as it hit the far stone wall.

"Hey! Leave him alone!" she shouted.

Her uncle ignored her and dragged the man/beast up from the floor. He quickly secured the man's hands. As she watched, she saw his body transforming slightly as he shifted to his human form. What had once been claws were now huge, regular, though still sooty, feet.

"Finish with her now," Claudius snapped at the nameless vamp still drawing her blood.

Her uncle kept his gaze on the newest prisoner. "You are definitely a welcome surprise. Don't get too comfortable," he murmured to the growling man in that creepy, evil way of his.

The vampire pulled the IV from her arm and on trembling legs stood and gathered everything. The stench of his fear was even more potent now. She wanted to tell him to grow a pair.

As he left the cell, Claudius stood there, watching them like the megalomaniac he was. Like he was a king and they were his peasants or something. "Did you speak to her?" Claudius asked in a voice so eerily calm it sent a chill snaking down her spine.

The vamp cleared his throat. "No."

Wrong answer. She knew it before he'd uttered the lie.

Claudius plucked the blood bag from the vamp's hand, passed it to a waiting lackey lurking in the main doorway, then sliced off the other vamp's head in one clean sweep using razor sharp claws. Vega had never seen anyone do something like that before.

She'd never seen a lot of stuff until she decided to run away to meet her dad. Closing her eyes, she filed that sight away with crap she never wanted to witness again. When she opened them again, the vamp was a pile of ash.

"You can blame yourself for his death." Claudius still stood there and she wanted nothing more than to wipe that imperious smirk off his face.

She shrugged as much as her chains would let her. "I didn't kill him."

Those dark eyes narrowed. "Perhaps you are more like your mother than I thought."

"I'll take that as a compliment."

His jaw tightened at that. "I'm going to torture and kill her in front of you. We'll see how arrogant you are then."

Vega snorted with a lot more confidence than she actually had. She didn't want this maniac anywhere near her mom. "My father will you kill you before that." She felt like a five year old kid on the playground telling another kid that her dad could beat up their dad. In this case, all she had were rumors to go on, but she'd heard how powerful Finn Stavros was. And she didn't even know if her mother would find her in time. Vega was just hanging on to a thread of hope that she would.

Maybe it was her imagination, but Claudius paled a fraction. Instead of responding, he pulled the heavy iron door shut behind him. A dull echo filled the room as the lock clicked back into place.

Vega turned to look at the chained man through the bars of their adjoining cells to find bright silver eyes staring at her. They were so vivid, made even more so against his dirty face, she sucked in a breath. She couldn't even tell how old he was. Not with all that dirt. He was big though, definitely over six feet. His arms and legs were freaking huge. "Are you okay? Where did you come from?" she whispered. She wasn't sure if her uncle had video cameras or recorders in here, but she hadn't seen any cameras at least.

He stared at her so long she didn't think he would answer. When he did, it surprised her. "Why did you tell him to leave me alone?" His voice was hoarse, as if he hadn't used it in ages.

She frowned, not understanding. "Why wouldn't I? Look, why are you here? Do you know either of my parents? What's your name?" Vega bit her tongue so she'd stop bombarding the filthy stranger with questions. He was clearly in worse shape than her.

"I...came through the gate that vampire opened. I don't know your parents and I don't have a name."

She was going to go back to the no name thing later, but first... "You came through the hell gate?" She hadn't seen it because she'd had a hood over her head, but she knew what her uncle was doing. He'd boasted about it practically nonstop on the drive to New Orleans. And she could smell the sulfur coming from outside their dungeon so she knew the hell gate was close.

He nodded.

"You don't look like a demon." The truth was, she hadn't actually seen one. She'd heard about them and read about them, but that was it.

He laughed bitterly, the sound raspy. "I'm not. We need to get out of here."

"No kidding." She tugged on the silver chains, her inner wolf howling in agony as the silver scraped against her wrists, the metal chafing. "Until I get my strength back that's not an option. And if they keep taking my blood, I won't be able to get stronger."

He looked around their cells, at the ceiling, walls, and metal doors as if assessing everything. Then he pinned her with that silvery gaze again. The brightness had faded a little so they were grayer now. "Don't scream," he whispered.

Why would she scream? Before she could ask, he opened his mouth and released a long stream of scorching orangey-red flames.

CHAPTER TWELVE

With his back pressed up against the high stone wall surrounding the two-story mansion in the Garden District, Finn waited for the signal. Impatiently.

The ever resourceful Spiro had given all of his team—including the two vamps from Lyra's former coven—earpieces and locked them into the same frequency. He scented other vamps nearby, but couldn't be sure this was the place they were looking for. The vampire Bruno could have lied about the location.

Finn didn't think he had, but the vamp's fear had been so strong it could have overpowered the stench of a lie. With fear like that, however, it was a good bet this was the place.

Right now he couldn't afford to be wrong. Not with his daughter's life hanging in the balance.

"Four vamps visible. One on the east perimeter near the wall, two in the backyard and one on the far south corner leaning against a tree. There might be more. Trees are too thick." Lyra's voice was so low he wouldn't have heard her without the earpiece. She was too high in the air, using her ability to fly to give them a perfect aerial view.

Considering they were moving in practically blind, her gift was the best option they had right now to infiltrate this place unseen. Gabriel had rounded up five warriors in addition to the four others who had been searching with him in Biloxi yesterday. He hadn't expected them to come since they were running on practically no sleep, but according to his Guardian they'd insisted. Word had spread that he had a daughter and the entire pack had wanted to come to New Orleans to help.

A daughter.

Fuck, he had to keep his head on straight. "I'll take the east, everyone else, you know what to do." They'd been in enough battles with other supernatural beings over the decades and fought alongside each other enough that he didn't need to give explicit instructions. His men and women were trained well.

They would secure the perimeter, then move on the house. From there, they would take down any other combatants who got in their way. Simple as that. Victoria was waiting in one of the vehicles in case they needed her healing strength. If Vega was hurt—he cut down that thought with a razor-sharp blade.

Using all the strength in his legs, he jumped up nine feet and grabbed onto the outer edge of the wall. Then he pulled himself up and crouched low, scanning the expansive yard. Magnolia and oak trees covered the property.

Below him he spotted the vamp Lyra had been talking about. On his cell phone, the vamp was texting. Shaking his head, Finn jumped down and unsheathed his claws in midair. The vamp must have heard him because he turned, shock on his face.

He dropped his phone and went to grab for a blade sheathed against his hip, but Finn struck hard and fast, slicing through the man's neck. Normally he preferred to fight in wolf form, but that wasn't the best option tonight. He needed to be fast and deadly. There was no margin for error.

Seconds later the vamp turned to ash at his feet. An unfamiliar scent teased his nose. Turning, ready to strike, he stopped as Lyra dropped from the sky, bringing her blade down on his would-be attacker in a perfect slice. The female vamp's eyes widened a split-second before her head tumbled to the ground. Just as quickly, her body disintegrated into ash.

"Thanks," he murmured to her. Seeing her like this now reminded him of how much she'd changed. She'd been strong before, but now she was also trained to kill quickly and efficiently. Something that shouldn't turn him on, but did. "Everyone check in," he ordered, whisper quiet.

Once he received affirmative responses that everyone was alive and the perimeter was secure, he motioned toward the house. "Move in."

He and Lyra headed for the east side of the house where there was a small iron fence that wrapped around a descending staircase. There was also a door that led into what he guessed was a kitchen or utility room, but the stairs led below ground into what could be a basement. And basements in the South were almost unheard of. Especially in below sea level New Orleans with hurricanes and flooding. One would have to be completely insulated.

"Moving in behind you with Rhea and Solon," Gabriel murmured through his earpiece. "Leaving a team of three in the yard and four others infiltrating the house."

"Good." Finn looked at Lyra as they descended the long flight. From the yard this would have been difficult to spot, but Lyra had seen it from her aerial view. He stopped in front of what had once been a door.

A giant hole had burned away most of it, leaving only hinges and scraps of wood hanging from the frame. The smell wasn't sulfuric. Not demonic fire. It was unique.

"What did this?" Lyra whispered, though he didn't think she was looking for an answer. Right now she was practically vibrating with energy. Her grayish-violet eyes were bright with hope and stark fear. Next to him Lyra tightened her grip on her blade and nodded at him. *Go*, she mouthed.

Tense and alert, he stepped through the opening. With his shifter-sharp eyesight he could see another opening about twenty feet in front of them, but he wanted to make sure the area wasn't rigged with traps. There were new smells in the stone hallway. A wet, cold scent and underneath it was sulfur. Not from the fire though. The sulfur lingered in the air and it was getting stronger the farther they moved in.

The narrow stone hallway had a high ceiling, probably around twelve feet. Likely went all the way up to the bottom of the house. Once they reached the end of the hallway, his wolf was clawing at him, begging to be set free.

The sulfur was almost overpowering now but all down the hallway he'd smelled roses too. It permeated everything, making his most protective side flare to life in a way he'd never imagined possible. The need to protect his child was making his wolf insane. Vega was here. Or had been.

Carefully, he stepped through the entryway, his gaze sweeping the surroundings of the underground area in seconds. It was one big stone room with candles everywhere, on the walls, the floor, various pedestals. Some were knocked over, extinguished while others still flickered.

And in the middle was a fucking hell gate.

Dark mist swirled in a perfect circular formation, a big black area that looked almost viscous smack dab in the middle of the room. Floating in the air. Only a curved quarter section of the black circle was open, in the shape of a crescent moon. Wisps of smoke curled out of it in addition to that God awful sulfuric stench.

Blood had been smeared on the ground in different designs he didn't recognize, but he could guess what they were for.

"Akkadian ritual spells. I can't believe he's really opening this," Lyra murmured as she stepped past him, eying the floor in horror. Pain and rage rolled off her in equal measures, mirroring his own feelings. Where was Vega?

He wanted to stop her, to shield her from all this, but kept pace as she moved around the hell gate toward the other side of the room.

"Everyone be careful." Just because the gate wasn't fully open didn't mean anything. He'd never been in a situation like this before and wanted his packmates safe. For all he knew it could split wide open at any second, without the coming eclipse. He hated the uncertainty.

No one said anything, but he heard them moving behind them. As they moved, he spotted a door completely melted away on the other side. The scent of roses was strong, permeating the air.

"Vega," Lyra said, moving into action before he could stop her. With a burst of speed, she was across the room in a heartbeat.

He was right behind her, moving through the entryway only a second after her. He froze at the sight. There were three cells. Arm and leg chains from two of them had been burned off the walls and a hole burned through the middle of two connecting cells and through one of the prison doors.

He could smell Vega all over the room. Lyra let out a cry as she ran to the front of the middle cell. Clutching onto the bars, she crushed them to dust as she stared inside. "She was here. Something bad happened here." Her voice was broken.

Finn pushed down his own pain and fear as he reached for her. She didn't shove him off. Letting out a sob, she turned her face into his chest and clutched onto his shirt. "This is all my fault," she whispered, the raw agony in her voice a knife through his chest.

He wrapped his arms around her, crushing her to him. She felt so small in his embrace, so delicate even though he knew firsthand just how strong she was. The wolf demanded he protect his female, do whatever it took to erase her pain. "No it's not. And we're going to find her." Or he would die trying. He hadn't scented Vega in the yard, only once they reached the hallway, but that didn't mean anything. They had a big group and would hunt the entire city for her. "There are still hours until sunlight."

Lyra immediately straightened at his words, wiping the pinkish tears from her face as she pulled back. "You're right."

If they didn't reach her by sunrise, they'd only have one more day and night to find her before the eclipse. After that...he couldn't even go there.

CHAPTER THIRTEEN

Lyra picked up a vase on the nightstand and hurled it across the room. It shattered into a million pieces, the blue porcelain glittering on the hardwood floor like rain. The destruction might not serve any purpose but it made a small part of her feel better.

A second later, the door flew open. Finn stood shirtless in the doorframe, looking ready to kill. He scanned the room and stilled when he saw the remains of the vase. He scrubbed a hand over his face, clearly as exhausted as she felt. Probably more so considering he'd been running on no sleep.

They'd scoured the city until Lyra had been forced inside by the damn sun. Finn's pack owned multiple homes in New Orleans. One in the French Quarter and two in the Garden District. He'd brought her to one in the Garden District then left immediately, continuing in the search for Vega. She was thankful he'd continued to hunt, but she hated feeling helpless.

Useless.

She was going crazy not knowing where Vega was. Where had she been taken? Or gone to? That scene in those cells was too strange. After Lyra had almost had a breakdown she'd eyed the area more critically. With the way the bars had been melted, it was clear something had broken out. After burning through Vega's chains.

The scent of Vega's blood still taunted her. Was it from being burned or from being drained? Either way didn't matter because neither option was good. Now some of Finn's packmates were guarding that mansion in case anyone else showed up. He'd called in more reinforcements from Biloxi once they'd gotten a good look at that hell gate.

"I'm sorry about the vase," she muttered.

He shook his head. "It doesn't matter. Have you slept at all?"

"No." She kept seeing Vega in pain when she closed her eyes. Her imagination just conjured up all sorts of bad things.

He looked out into the hall, then back at her and she could see he was torn. "I need to recharge. My wolf is threatening to take over and unless I get a couple hours of sleep I'm going to do something I won't be able to take back."

She understood. With his lack of sleep for so many days, he might be likely to turn into a wolf on a crowded human street. That wouldn't do anyone any favors. "Sleep. I won't make any more noise. I swear." She needed to try again too. The sun would be setting soon and when it did, she was heading back out there.

He shut the door behind himself and stepped farther into the room.

She frowned. "What are you doing?"

"We need sleep and we'll find it easier with each other." As he spoke he stripped off his clothes.

Beyond surprised by his assumption, she stepped back. "Are you kidding me?" Even if she did feel safer in his arms she didn't want sex right now.

He pinned her with that gaze. "Do I look fucking hard to you? I just need to sleep and for some reason both me and my wolf rest better with you in my arms." His words came out as an angry growl.

She sucked in a breath at his admission. The truth was, she did too. Always had. Seventeen years hadn't diminished that. Wordlessly, she turned from him and headed toward the queen-sized bed. As she slipped into bed, she felt him move right in behind her.

The sheets were soft and cool, but he was like a furnace, warming her from the inside out as he pulled her back to rest against his chest. His muscular arm wrapped snugly around her, his breathing steady as his chin settled on the top of her head. She could feel his warm breath on her hair.

Despite the panic and fear living inside her, his hold was grounding. Comforting.

"I never wanted to end things between us. My uncle had been growing more unstable and...I think he suspected I'd met someone. He'd had me followed a few times. For a while it was easy to lose my tails, but it was getting harder and harder to meet up with you unseen." Finn's deep voice filled the silence of the curtain-darkened room.

His words took her off guard, unraveling her at the seams. When he'd ended things between them, they'd fought bitterly. She remembered it as if it was yesterday. Even then he'd told her that he hadn't wanted to break up with her, but hearing the words now demolished the rest of the wall she had surrounding her heart. She swallowed hard, not sure how to respond. But she tightened her hand over his where it lay across her middle.

"Living without you was hell," he whispered. His grip tightened as he pulled her close. "I took on any challenger our pack had. It was like I was possessed with the need to destroy. I was just so damn angry you were gone." His harsh laugh was tinged with bitterness. "Ironically that's when I started gaining supporters in the pack and what ultimately gave me the strength to challenge him."

"Was it hard to take over the pack?" Finn had always been so damn strong. Stronger than even he'd realized. But she'd known it years ago and could definitely see it now. He was a true leader who looked at all angles. He cared about what was best for his pack.

"It was rough for a few years trying to figure out who could be trusted. Once I weeded out those with archaic ideals, it was easier to start growing all of our businesses. My uncle had kept everyone in the dark about finances, kept everyone working for pennies. Now the pack owns everything equally. It's the way it should be."

If all the homes his pack owned and his hotels she'd seen on the way into Biloxi were any indication, they were clearly doing well. "I really am sorry I never told you about her. I just...I didn't know what the right decision was back then. You'd been so sure we couldn't make it and...even though I was angry at you and wanted to deny what you said, I was afraid. I'd been sensing your growing fear of your uncle and I was terrified for our child. I already knew she'd have a hard enough time being a hybrid." She could still remember the fear and pain she'd experienced the day she'd been kicked out into the human world on her own. She'd been more sheltered than she'd even realized. Reality had been a swift punch in the face once she'd had to hide that first day for shelter from the sun.

His grip tightened. "No more apologies. I don't know what I'd have done in your shoes."

"Finn—"

"No more. I don't hate you if that's what you're worried about. I'm angry that I've missed so many years of

Vega's life, but we're going to find her and I'm going to make up for lost time."

Yes, he would. He deserved it and would have been a wonderful father to Vega all these years. While she was grateful he didn't despise her, he hadn't mentioned any other feelings. Not that she really expected him to. But she could hope, even if that hope might kill her. "Can I ask you something?"

"Yeah," he murmured, his voice a deep caress wrapping around her.

"I have no right to ask, but..." Oh, God. Why was she asking this? "Is it true you haven't taken a lover since we've been separated?" Seventeen years was long, but not that long to supernaturals. She truly had no right to ask, but Victoria's words to her had been rolling around in her head for days.

"There's been no one." His words shattered through her.

She closed her eyes. Damn. She might have been hoping for that answer, but she hadn't expected it. Not truly. Not for such a raw, sexual male like Finn. Knowing he hadn't been with anyone else sent an unexpected rush of heat between her legs. "I haven't either," she whispered. In the beginning she'd been consumed with taking care of her child and hiding her true nature from the human world. But once she'd made a stable home for her and Vega, the thought of anyone else's touch but Finn's had made her skin crawl.

Behind her, he went impossibly still. She could feel his heart rate increase and it was impossible to miss the sudden push of his erection against her back. "You shouldn't tell me that." She barely heard his words.

"Why not?" she asked just as quietly.

"When I thought...you'd had a child with someone else, my first instinct was to hunt him down and kill him. My wolf was dangerously close to taking over."

She might not have an inner animal to control in the same way he did, but she certainly had to control her baser instincts. At least where he was concerned. If she'd scented anyone on his sheets or in his bedroom...yeah, she didn't even want to go there.

Finn's hand played with the hem of her tank top, splaying across her belly. He moved across her skin slowly, almost as if he was asking for permission. The skin on skin contact made her nipples harden, the points rubbing against her cotton shirt.

His fingers slid lower, lower, until they dipped below the band of her thin sleep shorts. She wasn't wearing anything else and when he realized that, he sucked in a sharp breath. His fingers skated over her bare mound until he was cupping her possessively. Her inner walls clenched and tightened, wanting him to fill her. But he didn't go any farther or even stroke her folds or clit. He just held her.

"Tell me to stop," he growled, but she could tell he didn't want her to. His breath was warm against her neck, sending tingles down her spine. He rolled his hips against her once, pressing his hard length against her.

She should. They needed sleep and the sun would be setting soon. And once they crossed this line there would be no going back for her. The truth was, there was no going back now. She was completely lost over this male. "Don't stop," she found herself saying instead, the words torn from her chest.

Maybe she had a masochistic streak because there was no way things would ever work out between them and this would just make it harder to leave later. They were from two different worlds. Their people had a long, violent history of despising each other. Their relationship hadn't worked before... Could it now? She was afraid to even hope.

This wasn't about a relationship anyway, it was about finding escape until they could leave the house—that was the lie she was trying to tell herself.

It wasn't that simple for her, but she couldn't afford to assume this meant they had a future. She knew without a doubt that he still cared for her, probably loved her—otherwise, he'd have taken lovers since they'd been apart—but that couldn't negate that he was an Alpha and she was a vampire.

He growled softly and nipped her ear. Everything else fell away as he slowly started teasing her clit with his middle finger. Her entire body jolted at the feel of the rough pad against her sensitive bundle of nerves. She pushed back into him, rubbing her backside over his hard length as he teased her. And he was definitely teasing.

He knew her body well enough to realize that his gentle touch wasn't going to be enough. "Faster," she demanded.

Instead of doing what she wanted, he pulled away. Before she could protest, he flipped her on her back. With her heightened eyesight she could see the hard planes and striations of his perfectly chiseled body. Straddling her hips, his cock curved upward in a thick, impressive display she wanted to taste and touch.

Keeping her gaze on his, she reached out and grasped her fingers around his cock. His thick length was hot in her hands. She stroked him once, twice, savoring the way his entire body trembled as she touched him.

"Lyra." Her name was a prayer on his lips, reverent and strained at the same time.

Squeezing, she smiled when he rolled his hips into her grip.

Taking her off guard, he grasped her wrist and pulled her hand away. "I'm not coming in your hand."

Guiding both her hands above her head, he held her wrists in place in that impossibly firm grip as he bent his head down to meet hers. His lips brushed against hers, softly at first. With each stroke of their tongues, his kisses grew more demanding, hungrier. As if he wanted to completely devour her. To brand her.

Unable to move her hands, she arched into him, rubbing her breasts against his rock hard chest. Her nipples, already painfully erect, tingled with each contact, the friction making her crazy. It didn't matter that she still had the tank top on, it was so thin it might as well not even be there.

Her inner walls were clenching out of control, desperate to be filled. But Finn had her pinned down completely with his large body, his cock resting against her lower abdomen as he continued kissing her. Her shirt had pushed up so she felt his erection against her bare skin. It was almost more than she could take. She didn't want to feel him on her stomach, she wanted him claiming her in the way only he ever could.

She grinded against him, trying to encourage him to do more. The simple stimulation of her nipples was almost enough to send her over the edge. But it wasn't just that. It was Finn.

He was on top of her, holding her down, dominating her the way he'd done countless times years ago. He was Alpha everywhere, including in the bedroom. Especially in the bedroom. It was the one place she didn't mind his dominance. If anything, she craved it here. He always made her feel safe, treasured.

When he started feathering kisses along her jaw up to her earlobe, she rolled her hips against him again. She wanted to feel his thick length pushing deep inside her, wanted to drink his blood while they made love. They'd done it so often in the past and she missed it more than she wanted to admit.

But she didn't dare ask for that. He might have offered his neck to her before, but it had been because she needed it. For her to feed from him while they were making love would make him vulnerable and she didn't know if he was willing to do that. She was too afraid to ask.

When he started a path down her collarbone to the upper swell of her breast, his teeth nipping her skin, she lost what little control she had left.

"Fuck me," she whispered, knowing the reaction she'd get.

There was no way she could have contained the words. Couldn't have even if she'd wanted to. Her body craved his in a way that defied logic. It was like she'd been made for him. And him for her.

Letting her wrists go, Finn sat back. Breathing hard, he stared down at her, his blue eyes seeming to glow in the dark room. He'd been serious about how close his wolf was to the surface, ready to take over. She knew he was running on empty and needed a few precious hours of sleep. That, she could give to him. Later, if there was a next time for them, they could take things slow and relearn every inch of each other's bodies. But not now.

His eyes flared bright as he reached for her shorts. He practically tore them down her legs as she did the same to her top, frantically yanking it off and tossing it away.

Once she was completely bared to him, his stare went molten. "You're mine, Lyra." There was no control in his hoarse voice.

She nodded, not bothering to deny the truth. She was his and had been from the moment she'd stepped into that shifter bar so many years ago. He owned her heart and soul. She knew that made her ten kinds of stupid, but she didn't care.

He cupped her mound in that possessive way of his, dragging his finger along the length of her wet slit. When he slid two fingers inside her, testing her slickness, he shuddered, but didn't take his eyes off hers.

Moving away, he pulled back before settling his cock between her legs. His hard length pushed at her wet opening, but didn't fully penetrate.

"Don't tease." She couldn't take it. Her inner walls tightened, knowing what was coming.

Inch by inch he pushed inside her, his thickness filling her completely until she forgot to breathe.

Growling, he buried his face against her neck. He scraped his canines against her soft flesh. "You feel amazing."

He did too, but she couldn't find her voice. But she could show him what she needed. For him to move. Clutching onto his shoulders, she rolled her hips.

He growled again and they found a steady rhythm as he thrust harder with each stroke. Each time he pushed deep inside her, her already building climax raced closer to the edge of that cliff.

"Feed from me." His strangled demand slammed through her.

She couldn't believe what he'd said but she wasn't going to question it. She'd been keeping her fangs in out of fear she'd take what her body was demanding without his permission. His demand set her free.

Releasing them, she sank her teeth into his neck the instant he tweaked her clit. As she sucked deep, his sweet blood coating her tongue and running down her throat, her orgasm surged through her.

The sharpness of it took her by surprise. Hitting all her nerve endings at once, she lost all control as she was consumed by pleasure. She was filled with him, both his body and his blood, surrounded by his scent and his strength.

"Lyra." There he went again with that low, sexy voice.

He continued thrusting as his climax built, his movements now unsteady and out of control. She knew he was going to come the moment before he let go. His entire body, including his neck muscles, pulled tight as he shouted her name. She sucked harder against his neck, knowing the reaction it would elicit, the intensified pleasure it would bring him.

He groaned even louder as he continued slamming against her until they both collapsed, boneless. She licked the small puncture wounds, though they were already healing. She just wanted to taste him more, couldn't seem to make herself stop.

He simultaneously nuzzled her neck, murmuring her name under his breath. It sounded so much like a prayer that tears sprung to her eyes. She quickly blinked them away as sleep set in. Staying wrapped around him, she said, "Sleep, Finn."

He rolled to the side, tugging her with him as he moved. She curled up against him, soaking up his warmth as she let sleep overtake her. It touched her on the deepest level that this powerful Alpha trusted her enough to sleep in the same bed, to make himself even more vulnerable with her. She tightened her grip

around him, taking advantage of their limited time together. As she started to doze she could hear his breathing even out. Good. In a few hours God knew they'd
need it because she was going to rip this city apart until
she found Vega.

CHAPTER FOURTEEN

Lyra jerked up in bed at the low ringing sound, panic thrumming through her. Finn was gone and her internal clock told her sunset was maybe half an hour away. She snatched her phone off the nightstand and frowned at the number. She didn't recognize it, but for all she knew it could be one of Finn's packmates or he was using another phone.

"Hello?"

"Mom?" Vega whispered, her voice shaky.

"Vega!" she shouted, then cringed. "Honey, where are you?" Lyra grabbed her discarded pants from the antique chair in the corner of the room and started tugging them on.

"In a graveyard. I had to steal a phone from a human groundskeeper using mental persuasion. Then I told him to go home and forget he ever saw me."

She didn't care if Vega had out and out mugged someone. She just needed her daughter's location. "What graveyard?"

"I'm not sure where we are," she whispered again. "Claudius had me and another prisoner in chains. The prisoner helped us both escape but he's hurt and we're both exhausted. We...ran as far as we could but it wasn't far. I don't think any of his people followed us though because it was right at sunrise. I wanted to call you earlier, but we passed out. I barely managed to drag us into one of the empty vault tombs but mom, this guy is hurt and I'm exhausted. I can't get him to wake up. We've got to help him and we both need blood bad."

Lyra grabbed her shirt, blade, shoes and jacket as she sprinted out the bedroom door. Keeping the items gathered against her chest, she raced down the hall, following the scents of the others in the house to guide her. "Can you see any kind of landmark? Is there any unique architecture in the cemetery? What stands out?" She barreled into the kitchen downstairs to find Finn, four of his packmates and Justus and Christian strapping on weapons. She mouthed Vega's name as she pressed speaker and put the phone on the marble island. Lyra tugged her rumpled shirt on as the room quieted.

"Hold on," Vega said.

Next to Lyra, Finn stared at the phone and gripped the island top until it cracked.

"She escaped with another prisoner and is in a cemetery but doesn't know where they are. She's trying to figure out her location," she murmured even though Vega would hear. She wanted her daughter to concentrate on her surroundings.

DARKNESS AWAKENED | 197

"Okay, I see a lot of vault tombs. There are too many to count..." She trailed off for a moment and Lyra thought of something else.

"Didn't you say you stole this phone from a groundskeeper?" she asked.

The moment she spoke, Lyra watched out of the corner of her eye as Spiro flipped open one of the three laptops on the counter. Without pause, he moved to the phone and looked at the caller ID before hurrying back to his computer.

"Yeah!" Vega sounded excited now. "He was wearing a green and white uniform. It had...crap, I can't remember what the patch on his shirt said." Her voice started to waver and Lyra knew she was trying not to cry.

"Honey, we're going to find you, I swear. One of your father's packmates is doing some magic on his computer right now." She looked at Finn as she spoke. His jaw was clenched tight but she could see the determination on his face as he met her gaze.

"I've got his billing address...his city of residence...hold on..." Spiro's fingers flew across the keyboard and Lyra watched as a social media site popped up. "Got his current place of employment!" More typing and another screen popped up. "And from the cemetery website, the picture of their employees' uniforms matches her description. This is the place."

"Did you hear that? We're on our way," she said as she watched Spiro pull up different maps.

"Please hurry." She sounded so young and vulnerable and Lyra wanted to kill her brother in that moment for putting Vega through hell. But more than anything she just wanted to save her daughter.

"It's isolated and not far from here," Spiro murmured as he mapped out a path from their current place to the cemetery.

"We're going to find you, Vega," Finn said, his voice thick with emotion.

When her daughter didn't respond Lyra took the phone off speaker and looked at Finn. "Go. I'll leave as soon as the sun sets."

He nodded, though he was already moving toward the door, looking fierce and determined. As he hurried away, he pulled out his cell phone and started barking orders into it, letting other packmates know where to head. Everyone except Justus and Christian raced out the door.

Lyra stayed on the line with Vega. "I'll be leaving in ten minutes. I'll fly so it won't take me long. After that I should be there in five." If her guesstimate from the open map view on the laptop was any indication it wouldn't take long.

"I believe you…I'm sorry I didn't say anything to him. I just got tongue-tied."

"Don't worry about that. Did you escape from the basement of a house with cells in it?" And a hell gate, but she didn't want to ask that just yet.

"Yes, but there was more there too. Mom, there was a hell gate and ritualistic stuff. It was scary."

"How did you escape? What happened to Claudius?" Maybe her brother was dead.

Vega paused. "Can anyone else hear you?"

Lyra met Justus's gaze. "Two vampires can. They're honorable though and won't repeat anything you say." She put a deadly bite behind the words. So far she believed them, but at this point she was still being cautious.

Both vamps nodded. "We swear."

"Did you hear that?" Lyra asked her daughter.

"Yes. Claudius was injured but not killed. And...please don't freak out but I was shot a couple times. So was the man who rescued me."

Lyra sucked in a sharp breath and forced herself to remain calm. No wonder they hadn't been able to get far. "How are you now?"

"Healed. Both of us. They were lead, not silver. Our bodies pushed the bullets out but that's why we couldn't go far and why we must have lost consciousness. We're just lucky no humans saw us."

"I'm so sorry, Vega. This is my fault." It probably wasn't the time for apologies, but she had to say it. As she spoke she strapped her blade on. "I should have let you go to see your father when you wanted."

Vega sniffled. "No, I should have listened. I just didn't want to wait one stupid week for you to contact him and make arrangements. I should have been patient. This is my fault."

Lyra shook her head even though her daughter couldn't see her. She started tugging her boots on. "*None* of this is your fault. Now tell me how you two escaped." The leftover scorch marks and burned out doors could mean any number of creatures, none that she could think of that were good.

"You can't tell anyone... Can you find some privacy?"

Lyra looked at the other two vampires and raised her eyebrows. Wordlessly they nodded and disappeared out of the room. She trusted them not to eavesdrop. "Okay, it's just me now."

Vega pushed out a harsh breath. "The man who saved me came out of the hell gate. I thought maybe he was a demon at first but...he's a dragon," she whispered the last part. "Before he passed out he made me promise not to tell anyone. But you don't count. Just please—"

"No one else will know." Shock rippled through her, but Lyra didn't care if a flying hedgehog had saved her daughter. All that mattered was Vega had escaped. "Did he injure Claudius?" It had to be the only way they'd managed to get out.

"He burned a couple of Claudius's vamps to ash and managed to graze Claudius before they opened fire on us. We still made it outside and from there he flew us a few miles until the sun started coming up. He wasn't able to fly very high before we basically crashed. I was in so much pain so I can only imagine he was worse. He...took most of the bullets for me, Mom. God, we've got to save him." Vega started crying then, the sound echoing from the vault tomb she was in.

"We will," Lyra said as she tugged her jacket on. "I'm keeping the line open and will leave this in my pocket, but I've got to go now. I love you."

"I love you too."

Lyra shoved the phone in her pocket then quickly found the other two vamps waiting near the front of the house. When Justus saw her, he handed her a gun which she tucked into the back of her pants. She didn't mind being over prepared with weapons right now. Without any further conversation, she yanked open the front door and raced outside. While the other two headed toward the driveway where an SUV waited for them, Lyra ran down the side of the house toward the backyard. Once she was sure she wasn't being watched by nosey humans, she took to the air, using the cover of night to hide her.

"Did you hear that?" Vega whispered to the unconscious, naked man with no name curled up in their cramped hiding spot. She set her phone down on the marble slab next to him. "Of course you didn't," she muttered, hating the fear that had taken over.

After being shot three times—which was another one of her new experiences she was going to pretend never happened—she'd tried so damn hard to stay awake once they'd found shelter. But that had freaking hurt. It didn't matter that she was supernatural and could heal faster, metal ripping through her flesh and bones sucked any way you looked at it. Now she felt as if she'd run back-to-back marathons. After losing so much blood beforehand she was just glad she was alive.

"We're going to be okay," she whispered again as she placed her palm over the man's forehead. His temperature was so high she wasn't sure how he could survive without help. Even though she was weak, she scored her wrist with her fangs and held it up to his mouth.

He moaned and moved against the stone floor as he slowly drank, but he still didn't open his eyes. So far their hiding place was working out pretty good. The cemetery the dragon shifter had flown them to was quiet, not like the touristy ones she'd read about. She'd been unconscious most of the day while her body healed itself so if there had been a lot of visitors she hadn't heard any of them from inside the tomb.

She still felt bad about stealing that guy's phone after she'd gone looking for help, but—she straightened at a very faint sound. Almost like a rustling outside.

Removing her wrist from the shifter's mouth, she stood up as much as she could. Because of the vaulted top she had a little room, but was still hunched over. Moving toward the marble slab covering, she turned her ear and listened.

When it cracked down the middle, she scrambled back, her heart in her throat. That sulfuric stench invaded her senses as she moved to cover the shifter's body. Even though she was weak she let her claws extend. She might not be able to shift to her wolf, but she wasn't letting anyone take her again. No freaking way.

The covering suddenly ripped away. Behind her, she felt the dragon moving, but she kept her focus on the opening. Moonlight streamed in as her uncle appeared in the dome opening.

He smiled evilly, his perfect features so at odds with the dark aura that clung to him like an oily film. "Stupid bitch. You can't escape me. I tagged you the moment I took you," he snarled.

Tagged? What the hell did that mean? Before she could respond an enraged howl rent the air. It was so loud, so *primal*, it sent chills down her spine. Multiple howls immediately followed, the sound music to her ears no matter how freaking scary. It was her father's pack.

She knew it and so did Claudius. He let out a vicious curse then looked to the side, away from her and out of her line of sight. "Stay with them. If they try to leave, kill them," he commanded.

In a blink he'd disappeared from view. Tentatively she moved to the entrance but jumped back when two of the grossest creatures she'd ever seen stepped into view. With reptilian skin and yellow eyes she immediately knew what they were.

Akkadian demons.

She also knew that her blood supposedly had the ability to control them. Now she had to figure out how and put it to use.

CHAPTER FIFTEEN

L yra's fear skyrocketed out of control as she skimmed the top of the oak trees. Vaulted domes and gravestones lined the expansive cemetery as far as she could see. She pulled her phone out of her pocket. The wind whipped around her as she scanned the area. "Vega?" she whispered.

No answer.

A moment ago she'd heard the howls of Finn's pack but then everything had gone silent. There were too many trees in the cemetery blocking her view. From the map she knew it expanded for a couple miles.

As she scanned the graves below her, a flash of glowing yellow caught her eye. She focused on it and made out two reptilian forms.

Withdrawing her blade, she continued her silent descent, her focus laser-sharp. Two Akkadian demons hovered in front of a vaulted grave. Large chunks of marble littered the ground as the demons looked at each other. It was almost as if they were communicating something, but with the direction of the wind she couldn't hear well enough.

Didn't matter.

She couldn't see anyone else around as a possible threat. Raising her blade high, she increased her descent. The two creatures didn't even hear her as she swooped down. She sliced at the first one, severing its head in one perfect move. Using her momentum she struck again, slicing off the next one's head.

As her feet hit the ground she turned in all directions, looking for more possible threats. The sulfur smell of the demons covered everything, making it impossible to scent anything else.

"Mom?"

Lyra swiveled again at the sound of Vega's voice. A second later Vega ducked out of the tomb the dead demons lay in front of.

Rumpled, her hair dirty, clothes ripped and covered in dried blood, Vega was the most beautiful sight Lyra had ever seen. Before she realized she'd moved into action, she had her blade sheathed and her arms wrapped tightly around her daughter. Her throat clenched as she choked back tears. Vega was safe and in her arms. The relief she experienced was so potent it almost knocked her off her feet. But she knew she couldn't relax yet. Not until her daughter was truly out of harm's way.

"Mom, you're suffocating me," Vega said, half-laughing, after a few moments.

Immediately Lyra pulled back. She cupped her daughter's cheek, but froze at a scuffling sound from inside the tomb. Shoving her daughter behind her, Lyra whipped out her blade again.

Two silver eyes stared at her out of the darkness. Even with her supernatural eyesight, it was hard to make out the big, hulking form. It was almost like the creature was blurred or something.

"He's okay mom, but he needs help," Vega said from behind her. She tried to step around her, but Lyra held up her blade-free hand.

"You saved my daughter?" she asked the male.

"Yeah," he rasped out, his voice strained. When he stepped into the moonlight she saw that he was naked and covered in dirt and possibly soot from head to foot. And he was huge. Seriously huge. He looked like he was in his early thirties, but in her experience that didn't mean anything. Not with supernaturals.

When he stumbled forward and groaned in pain, instinct kicked in. This male had saved her daughter from Claudius and deadly demons. She would help him. "Stay behind me, Vega," she ordered as she reached out and wrapped an arm around the male's waist.

She helped lower him to the ground. Her hand came away covered in soot. He moaned in pain as he practically collapsed against the outer wall of the stone tomb. Lyra reached into her pocket and tossed a pack of matches to Vega who was biting her bottom lip as she watched the dragon shifter. "Set the demons on fire. I'm going to feed him, then we need to get you two out of here." She also needed to find Finn and his pack, but right now she could only take one step at a time. Getting Vega to safety mattered more than anything and she knew Finn would want her to take care of their daughter.

Vega nodded and as she lit a match, Lyra opened a vein on her wrist. "Drink." Out of the corner of her eye, she saw the two demons burn to ash. In seconds, nothing remained of the creatures.

The male watched her with a guarded, skeptical gaze, as if he didn't understand what she was doing. "Listen buddy, you need to drink. My blood will help you and you need your strength so we can get you out of here." Because she knew her daughter wouldn't let her leave this male behind. Not that she would, even though every maternal instinct she had was screaming at her to fly Vega to safety.

"Please drink," Vega said softly from behind her.

After a pause, he latched onto Lyra's wrist and started sucking. His pulls were weak at first, but grew stronger as the seconds ticked by. When his grip on her arm tightened she thought she might have to fight to get her wrist back but he suddenly stopped.

Sniffing the air, he stood on steady feet, her blood clearly having done its job. He uttered a word she didn't understand. It sounded like a harsh, guttural language.

Then he said it again, this time louder, angrier. His muscular body was tense and everything inside Lyra went on alert. Without thinking she wrapped her arms around Vega and took flight, desperate to get her to safety.

As she hurtled higher through the air, she watched as the male below shifted into his dragon form. On a loud growl, his body transformed into an impossibly beautiful creature. Jade wings sparkled against the moonlight as if they were completely made of emeralds. And the wing span stretched higher, higher until she didn't even bother guessing how big he was. His body continued to grow, expanding until he had to take flight so he wouldn't destroy the vault tombs around him. What had once been human skin was now a glittering silver of beautiful diamond scales. The contrast against the jade colored wings was like nothing she'd ever seen before. The word beautiful didn't do him justice.

He flapped his wings, the sound echoing around them. Before she could blink, he'd all but disappeared and she could only see a blurry dark shape where he'd been. She'd read that ancient dragons had been like chameleons, able to change their body to blend in with their surroundings when they wanted.

When he started flying, the dark form blocking out the moon for a moment, Vega's grip tightened around her. "Follow him!"

Lyra started to say no. She needed to get Vega to safety and this dragon was leaving of his own accord. But the wind shifted direction, the scent of blood filling the air.

Finn's blood.

All around Finn, his packmates were battling with Akkadian demons and vampires. Though he couldn't see all of them because of the big tombs in the way he could hear them. Each victorious howl told him all he needed to know. His pack was winning.

Right now his focus was solely on Claudius Marius. Squaring off against him, the blond vamp had two blades in his hands. His hair was pulled back at his neck and he wore dark slacks and a crisp white shirt, as if he hadn't expected to fight tonight. Finn couldn't believe the vamp had been here, but he must have tracked Vega to the cemetery too.

He didn't care what the treacherous vamp's reason was for being there, Finn would take great pleasure in ending his life.

In his wolf form, everything around him was clearer, more focused.

Claudius lunged once, his left hand striking out with a blade as he tried to run it through Finn's chest. Finn jumped back and landed on all fours, the dirt and stone beneath his paws cold.

The vampire let out an angry snarl and jumped on a waist-high iron gate surrounding one of the tombs. He attempted to jump down at Finn and attack from above. When he did, he left himself vulnerable.

Lunging in a calculated move, Finn bit down on Claudius's calf. The vamp howled and stabbed him through the side. A glimmer of pain rippled through him, but he was so pumped up on adrenaline, he barely felt it. Letting go of Claudius's leg, he dropped to the ground but immediately dove over another iron gate with the blade still in him.

Shifting back to human form, he let out a howl of agony as he ripped the sword from his body. Almost immediately his body started healing itself. Keeping his focus on Claudius who now stood on top of one of the stone angels adorning a tomb, he hurled the sword in the opposite direction of the fighting and the vampire.

Taking one of the vamp's weapons was a psychological blow more than anything. He was going to keep chipping away pieces of the bastard until he was ash.

As he returned to his wolf form, a whoosh of air from above nearly blew him backward. Looking up, he growled and jumped over the gated area. A giant blur of *something* had just flown over him. When Claudius jumped onto the top of a nearby vault tomb in the direction the blur had just gone, Finn followed.

Keeping an eye on his surroundings for a surprise attack, he raced in and out of the maze of aboveground tombs, chasing after Claudius. He skidded to a halt as he spilled out into an open area of flat tombs where most of his packmates battled with vamps and demons. Some were using weapons, others were using claws. He scanned the area, looking for Claudius when a giant dragon materialized from out of thin air. One second there was nothing there, then the next a glittering beast was perched on top of two big vault tombs, using each as a foot hold.

What. The. Hell.

Finn leapt into action when the animal let loose a stream of scorching fire that lit up the dark night, illuminating the stone graveyard. His legs strained, eating up the distance as he raced across the flat open stone area to the other side. He had no clue if he could take the beast on, but he was damn sure going to try. All creatures had a weakness.

He stopped running only when he realized the dragon was burning demons and vampires in the direct vicinity of Victoria. With amazing precision. Anything that got too close to her was toast, but the creature was carefully avoiding her.

DARKNESS AWAKENED | 213

Finn wasn't sure what was going on or where that shifter had come from, but he remembered the strange scorch marks at Claudius's mansion. Maybe that was who Vega had escaped with. At this point the animal wasn't an enemy so he left him alone.

Swiveling as he scented Claudius, he ducked just in time to miss what would have been a decapitating blow. Rolling onto his back and away from the vamp, he quickly jumped onto all fours and faced off with him.

Claudius jumped away, putting distance between them as he continued to move.

Snarling, Finn raced toward the nearest raised tombstone. He jumped onto it, using it as a springboard to move to another one, then another one. After six fluid jumps, each one moving him closer and closer to Claudius, Finn launched himself at the vamp at the last second instead of diving for another tombstone.

The vamp, who had been tense and spinning in each direction Finn moved, brought his blade up to stab him through his chest. Finn twisted midair, using his agility, and latched onto Claudius's upper arm as he flew past him.

He didn't release the vamp as his momentum continued to propel him forward. He heard the pop then a ripping sound as sweet blood coated his tongue. As Claudius slammed against the ground, Finn released his arm and spun to face him again.

Claudius's scream filled the night air, his arm dangling by tendons. He snarled something incomprehensible, blood and spit flying out of his mouth. His arm would eventually heal—but he wouldn't live that long.

Finn went back on his haunches, poised to strike when another scream rent the air.

"Nooooooo!" He turned to see Lyra flying toward them, Vega in her arms screaming at the top of her lungs.

In human form, Gabriel was on one of the vault tombs behind the dragon, blades in hand, looking ready to attack the creature. *Shit.*

Finn let out a loud howl, signaling for his Guardian to stop. But it was too late. Gabriel launched himself through the air. Sensing the attack, the dragon turned and flapped out one of his huge glittering wings. He struck Gabriel with it, but his Guardian's blade sliced through the membrane of the wing. An angry screech echoed around them as the dragon spit a wild stream of fire into the air.

Out of the corner of his eye he saw Lyra flying away with Vega. *Thank God.* They needed her out of here.

Everything had happened in a matter of seconds, though it felt like an eternity. He'd kept Claudius in his peripheral and the cowardly vamp was trying to flee. Clutching his useless arm to his body, he'd jumped onto another vault tomb. Finn howled and took chase. As he launched himself onto one of the tombs, Claudius looked at him, then behind him—at Lyra and Vega.

With his good arm, the vamp hauled back and threw his blade in a high arc. Finn jumped to the nearest tomb, using it as a springboard, then flew at Claudius with all the power and speed he possessed.

The vampire tried to jump, but Finn read his body language clearly and adjusted his direction. As he reached the vamp he didn't waste time fighting with him. His jaws clamped down on the male's neck. Vaguely he was aware of claws digging into his ribcage, but he ignored it as he severed Claudius's head completely.

Blood filled his mouth as the ancient vampire turned to dust beneath him. With no time to revel in his victory, he turned and raced through the tombs, using Lyra's scent as a guide. The place had grown eerily silent, telling him the demons and vamps had to be dead.

The farther he ran, the stronger he could smell Lyra's blood and it was tearing him up inside. Had Claudius wounded her? Or worse? No, no, *no*.

When he saw her lying on the ground, eyes closed, body impossibly still, he shifted to his human form mid-stride. Vega and Victoria knelt beside her and Gabriel was hovering a few feet away, his wary gaze on a hulking human male Finn assumed was the dragon shifter. As long as Gabriel and the male weren't fighting or getting in his way, he'd deal with that issue later. Lyra was all that mattered.

Victoria's hands were on Lyra's chest over a gaping wound. A soft blue glow emanated from her hands and the jagged wound. Finn felt as if his own heart had been pierced.

"What happened?" he rasped out as he knelt next to them. He wanted to touch Lyra so badly he ached for it, but didn't want to get in Victoria's way when she was doing her healing magic. He looked at Vega and was once again stunned by how much she looked like both him and Lyra. Seeing her in the flesh brought up so many damn emotions he had to shove them back.

Especially now.

"She took the hit so I wouldn't be struck..." Vega seemed to push the words out before breaking down sobbing. Even though they'd never spoken to each other he wrapped his arm around her shoulders and pulled her close. Sobbing, Vega buried her face in his shoulder. Even though he hated everything about this situation, it touched him on the deepest level that she'd turned to him for comfort. He just wished he'd been able to do more for her and Lyra.

His throat tightened as he watched Victoria and Lyra. He refused to lose her. Not now when he'd just found her again. Not when they could become the family he'd always dreamed of.

"Victoria?" he asked quietly, needing answers.

His healer didn't answer. Her eyes were closed in concentration. The glow spread all across Lyra's chest, up her neck and across her pale face. Inch by inch it covered her entire body. Even though she was mostly covered with clothing, the radiance was visible even under the dark material of her pants and top.

A low growl momentarily drew his attention away from her. He turned to find the dragon shifter staring at Victoria and rumbling low in his throat. For a second he thought the action was hostile then realized the male was making a warning sound. He was worried. Finn looked back at the two women and his pulse stuttered.

Lyra's wound was almost closed, but Victoria was pale and shaking. Shit. He hadn't even been paying attention to her. Shame filled him as he opened his mouth to order his healer to stop. But he couldn't find the words. Couldn't force them out. He needed Lyra to live. As Alpha he had to look out for the good of his pack, to think of everyone else's needs above his own. But he couldn't right now.

"Victoria, stop!" Gabriel demanded behind him.

At that moment Lyra's pale eyes popped open and she sucked in a sharp breath. Her gaze landed on Vega and she smiled in relief. Finn's heart lurched. Dropping his arm from Vega, he gathered Lyra in his arms, pulling her tight to his chest. She returned his embrace, her grip weak. "I'm okay," she whispered against his neck.

"Thank you, Victoria," he whispered, unable to squeeze out any more words. His throat was too tight with emotion. He'd almost lost Lyra.

"No sweat," Victoria laughed shakily and he watched as Gabriel helped her to her feet. The dragon shifter growled again, possessively this time, but Finn ignored that. For now. He was going to get his damn answers about who the male was.

His other packmates and the two vamps from Lyra's former coven had gathered around them and were all watching expectantly. He pulled slightly back so Vega could hug her mother. Keeping his arms protectively around both females, he looked at his men and women. "Is everyone accounted for?"

Everyone nodded, but Spiro spoke first. "All vamps and demons are dead. There are no humans in the direct vicinity. I can't say no one saw that fire-breathing light show, but a quick scan of the area says we're clear."

"Good. Take Christian and Justus with you and span out for two miles. Look for any witnesses." He looked at Justus next. "If anyone saw anything, make them forget."

The three nodded and moved into action. He focused on Gabriel next, ready to order him to get Victoria back to one of their homes so she could rest when the ground rumbled beneath them.

He increased his hold on Vega and Lyra as the earth shook ominously. Just as quickly as it started, it abruptly stopped.

Everyone looked at each other and he could feel Vega shaking against him and Lyra. He wanted to get both of them the hell out of there. Standing, he helped Lyra to her feet. She might be healed but the way she was clutching on to his forearm told him she was weak. Vega quickly moved to the other side of her mother, helping to hold her up.

"Anyone know what that was?" he asked, looking around the group. The South wasn't known for earthquakes but that was what it had felt like.

"It's the hell gate. Until it's closed, these rumblings will continue," the dragon shifter said.

"I thought it could only be opened during the eclipse," Vega said quietly, as she leaned closer to Lyra, wrapping her arm around her mother's shoulders.

"That's partially true. There are certain times of year when the veil between worlds is thinner."

"Like Halloween," Victoria interjected.

The male looked at her in confusion. "Halloween?"

"Ah, Samhain."

He nodded and focused on Finn again. "During eclipses, Samhain and other specific dates, the veil is thinner and hell gates can be opened with the right..." He appeared to struggle with the correct word, then said,

220 | KATIE REUS

"Circumstances." The dragon nodded at Vega. "Her blood has already started the process and if we do nothing it will remain cracked open. Eventually, eclipse or not, those on the other side will obliterate it. It could take months or even a hundred years, but until it's closed, that gate will always be a threat to the human world."

Finn wanted to know how the hell the guy knew all this. "You came from the gate?"

The stranger nodded.

"And you saved my daughter from the vampires?"

He nodded again.

Finn had more questions, but the fact that this male had saved Vega meant Finn owed him everything and would have to trust him. The male had even helped destroy vamps and demons in a battle he had no business joining. Something told him that had more to do with the way the male was possessively watching Victoria than anything, but he still owed this male. "Words aren't enough, but thank you. I am in your debt. How do we close the gate?"

The male looked at Vega. "We need her blood to do it."

CHAPTER SIXTEEN

"Hell no," Lyra snapped out with more energy than she actually felt. She would need Finn's blood soon or a couple days to rest in order to completely heal. Claudius's sword had pierced her heart—something that would have killed most vamps—but Victoria had started her healing process almost immediately. Combined with her strong bloodline, she was pretty sure that was the only reason she was still alive right now. Weak or not, no one was using her daughter for anything anymore. Even if it meant closing a hell gate. She tightened her arm around Vega's waist, pulling her closer.

"Just a little bit of blood. I didn't mean... I would *never* sacrifice anyone." The dark-haired male looked almost offended, but he was a stranger so it was hard to tell.

"Let's do it," Vega said next to her, sounding as exhausted as Lyra felt.

Lyra glanced at Finn first. He'd been sneaking glances at Vega as if in awe and when Lyra met his gaze she could tell he wanted to say no. Unfortunately they couldn't make that decision for her. Not if she was willing. She looked at their daughter. She was so damn strong standing there it made Lyra want to cry. Her daughter never should have had to go through any of this. "You're sure?" she asked.

Vega nodded. "Absolutely."

"How do we close it with her blood?" Finn finally asked.

The male paused for a moment, then spoke. "A short ritual chant while her blood is rubbed along the seam of the gate. Since that vampire used her blood to open it, we have to use hers to close it. And it has to be fresh."

"You know how to do the ritual chant?" Lyra asked.

He nodded, looking extremely uncomfortable as he glanced around at everyone. As if he was finally aware of the rest of the pack.

"Let's go then." Lyra wanted this over with. The sooner it was done, the sooner she could get Vega the hell away from New Orleans and this mess. Everything else, including her worries about her future with Finn, could take a backseat. She just wanted Vega safe.

Finn pointed at the dragon. "You're coming with us. I think I've got some extra clothes that might fit. Barely." When the male didn't argue, Finn looked at Gabriel. "Take Victoria and Lyra back to—"

The dragon shifter made that rumbling sound once again and looked at Victoria in a purely possessive manner that had everyone going still. *Holy crap.* Whatever was going on with him, he clearly wasn't letting the pretty shifter out of his sight. He didn't seem threatening and had gone out of his way to protect her, but still. His behavior was unnerving.

Victoria just stared at him with curiosity so she clearly wasn't scared. And Gabriel looked pissed, but he wasn't putting off possessive vibes toward Victoria. More like, big brother/little sister protection.

Lyra cleared her throat. They didn't have time for this situation to explode so she tried to quickly defuse it. "I'm not going anywhere with Gabriel and neither is Victoria. You can ride with us if you want. Is that okay?" she asked the female.

Victoria gave the dragon shifter a confused look before she nodded at Lyra. "Okay."

The male made a grunt of satisfaction, but Lyra ignored him. "Thank you for healing me, Victoria. I...I owe you everything." Lyra stumbled over her words, feeling so inadequate with the thank you.

The shifter's entire face tinged pink as if she was embarrassed, putting some color back into her cheeks, as she shook her head. "No, you don't."

Yes, she did, and Lyra hoped to show her thanks later. She didn't think there was a recipe for home-baked cookies that said 'thanks for saving my life from my crazy brother'. She couldn't cook anyway, but she was going to do *something* for Victoria. Right now, however, she realized that Victoria didn't like being the center of attention. Or she assumed that's why she seemed to be embarrassed.

Lyra started to respond when Finn let out a frustrated growl, interrupting them. She knew he didn't want her going with them, but she didn't care. She wasn't leaving her daughter's side again. And the truth was, she didn't want to leave Finn again either. She had no idea what the future held for them and she wanted to be with him for as long as possible.

"Fine, we're all riding together. What's your name, anyway?" Finn asked the male.

The dragon shifter looked like that proverbial deer caught in headlights for a moment. As if he didn't know the answer.

"His name's Drake," Vega said quietly.

Lyra knew when her daughter was lying and even though she wasn't putting off an acidic scent—either that or the freaking sulfur had simply coated everything—she knew Vega wasn't being truthful. She just wasn't sure why.

But the big male nodded in confirmation. "Drake."

"Gabriel, ride in the SUV with the team behind us," Finn ordered.

His Guardian looked as if he might argue, but nodded. He shot Drake a death glare. "I don't know what your deal is, but if you touch her, I'll fucking gut you." It was clear the 'her' referred to Victoria.

Drake's gray eyes flashed silver for a moment before returning to their muted color. "I would die before I hurt her or let anyone else." He gave Gabriel a condescending look that made it clear he viewed the Guardian as a non-threat before turning to Finn. "I would appreciate some clothes."

And that was that. Finn nodded and everyone moved into action.

Lyra kept her arm around Vega and headed out with the others. She knew Spiro and her former coven members would make sure the area was clear of humans but she didn't even care about that. When another, smaller rumble shook the earth, they all tensed and moved faster.

Finn kept a tight grip on Vega and Lyra's hands as they stood in the basement of Claudius's mansion. Drake was reciting a chant in a language Finn didn't recognize—which just added even more questions about who the hell this guy was—while Gabriel spread Vega's blood over the opening. He'd hated watching her cut her palm open, but Drake had been right that they only needed a little blood.

The more Drake chanted, the faster the crescent shaped opening slid closed. Angry cries from whatever creatures were behind the gate and additional smoke spilled out, but Drake increased his mantra until it closed. Though everything was silent, the black circle still hovered in the air. "Everyone stand back," Drake said, his body shuddering in exhaustion.

No one moved until Finn looked at his packmates and the two vampires who'd joined them, and nodded. "Move back."

As they did, Drake opened his mouth and let out a scorching stream of fire, encircling the black circular gate. A loud whooshing sound filled the air and in the blink of an eye, the gate was gone.

Silence descended on the basement/dungeon as everyone looked at each other. Drake turned and glanced first at Victoria, as if to make sure she was still there, then focused on Finn. "You should probably fill this area in and make sure it's not easily accessible."

He was already ahead of the guy, but nodded. Finn wasn't impressed by many people, but this shifter's ability to close the gate, as well as his fire-breathing, was incredible. "I will, thanks. Why were you in hell?"

Something dark passed over Drake's features, but he didn't answer. Okay, Finn would try a different tactic. "Do you know what year it is?"

He shook his head stiffly.

When Finn told him, the male's eyes widened slightly, but again he didn't respond. In the SUV on the way over, Finn had watched as he eyed the interior in an almost awed reverence. As if it was the first time he'd seen a vehicle. There was a lot Finn wanted to discuss with the male, but he also knew he shouldn't be doing it in front of everyone. If the guy had been in hell so long he didn't know what year it was, there was a big story there. Considering he was a dragon, Finn could imagine how he'd ended up below. Probably sacrificed because of his rare blood. His actions in the past few hours, however, had shown him to be an honorable male despite the cruel treatment he'd received from whoever had sent him to hell. "Until you figure out where you want to go or what you want to do, you're welcome to stay with my pack indefinitely."

The male eyed him warily. "In exchange for what?"

"Nothing. You saved my daughter. She's considered royalty on both my and her mother's side." Not that it mattered to Finn, but he hoped these were terms the male understood. Without knowing his history though, he was just guessing. "We owe you a huge debt that can never be repaid and offering you shelter will bring both of us honor." He would have offered to let the male stay anyway, but something told him Drake—or whatever his real name was—wouldn't take charity.

Drake relaxed a fraction, his hungry gaze straying to Victoria. She gave him a shy smile. "I live with the pack too."

That seemed to settle it because the dragon shifter nodded.

Finn caught his eye again. "We still have a lot to discuss."

There was no surprise in his expression. "I know."

Now that that was settled, he wrapped his arms around both Lyra and Vega, pulling them close as he faced his packmates and the two other vampires. It made him feel whole, somehow, having both females close against him. His daughter was an unexpected gift, and one he intended to cherish. "Seventeen years ago I made the biggest mistake of my life out of fear. Because of it, I lost something precious. That will never happen again. Those who stand here now declared loyalty to me before I killed my uncle and I hope I can count on that loyalty again when I take Lyra as my mate."

Both females stiffened against him, but he didn't look at either of them. For him, there was no question about what he wanted. Lyra at his side, and his daughter along with her. He needed his pack to understand how deeply he loved Lyra and he wanted them to know before they headed back to Biloxi. Because as soon as he made his intentions clear, word would spread to the rest of the pack like wildfire.

"You're the strongest among all of us." His gaze trailed over the male and female warriors bloodied and dirty before him. "If you have a problem with Lyra or my daughter, leave now and I'll let you go with no questions asked. But if anyone attempts to harm my mate or daughter in the future, you know what the penalty is." He didn't need to spell it out or make threats. They all knew and had seen him execute traitors before. And if someone came after his family, he'd make them sorry they were ever born.

No one moved except Gabriel. He went down on one knee, the act of subservience so out of character it stunned Finn. He bowed his head once to Lyra. "If you give Finn your loyalty, you'll have mine until death."

Like dominos, everyone in the room followed suit except the two vampires and Drake who quietly hung back. When Finn at last looked down at Lyra she had tears in her eyes. They turned his heart over. "Finn..." Trailing off, she swiped them away before meeting Gabriel's gaze. "No matter what, Finn will *always* have my loyalty."

He wanted more than that, he wanted her love. Years ago she'd claimed his heart. He wasn't sure if she realized that. Soon enough she would. But Finn understood that was a discussion for when they were in private and when his daughter and Lyra weren't so weak they were barely standing up. Right now he wanted both of them back at the mansion, safe under his roof. And once Lyra was rested, he was going to win her heart once and for all.

CHAPTER SEVENTEEN

Three days later

Lyra strode from Finn's bathroom, feeling refreshed after a long, hot shower. Not bothering with the lights in his room, she opened the drapes and let the moonlight illuminate everything.

The moon always soothed her, but right now she was edgy and only one thing would ease it. After everything Finn had said in that dungeon about making her his mate, he *still* hadn't broached the subject of it again. And it was starting to piss her off.

Of course she'd been pretty much laid up in bed healing and taking his blood for two days straight, but that didn't matter. While the feeding had inevitably turned her on, it had been more about sustenance. He'd stayed with her and held her after she'd fed each time, making her feel cherished. But, he hadn't been very talkative about the future.

Sighing, she opened the armoire that housed a massive flat screen television and turned it on. Ever since they'd returned to Biloxi she'd been keeping an eye on the news even though she knew Finn had left a few

232 | KATIE REUS

packmates in New Orleans to keep a pulse on the city and to completely fill in the basement where the hell gate had been. The various local stations and weather experts around the world had been fascinated by the earthquake and aftershocks in New Orleans. As she watched the screen, the door opened and Finn walked in looking good enough to eat.

Wearing cargo pants and a plain T-shirt that stretched across his perfectly muscular chest, he crossed his arms, drawing her gaze to his biceps. Her hunger instantly flared to life, her nipples straining against the thin fabric of her robe as heat rushed between her legs. After what they'd shared in New Orleans, it was like her body had flared back to life after a decades-long coma and it would not be appeased with anything but Finn.

Damn him and his sexiness.

For the past three days since they'd returned they hadn't done anything physical beyond kissing and her feeding from him. That didn't count. Not for how wired she was. Kissing was like throwing accelerant on a fire pit, then not lighting the match.

Somehow she smiled instead of jumping him. But only because she wasn't sure of his reception. Deep down she was worried he regretted making such a bold statement in front of so many packmates a few days ago. Hell, who knew what was going on in that frustrating male mind of his. "Hey. Looks like the news might have lost interest in the earthquake." She motioned to the screen where a perky reporter was talking about a breaking political scandal.

Finn just grunted a non-answer and stepped into the room, shutting the door behind him. She turned off the television and tossed the remote onto the bench at the end of his bed. With his gaze on her, he locked the door. For some reason, the clicking sounded almost ominous. His ice blue eyes swept down her entire body from head to toe as he took on a predatory stance she recognized.

Everything inside her tensed. She knew that look well, craved it.

"Vega's out shopping with Victoria. They're going to see a movie too," he said, breaking the expanding silence between them.

"I know. She texted me." Since they'd returned to Biloxi, Vega had been so busy it made Lyra's head spin.

After feeding from Lyra's wrist a couple times, she'd had had so much energy and was barely sleeping. They'd also had to remove a tracking chip that Claudius had embedded in her upper shoulder. Vega had told them Claudius had mentioned something about tagging her—which had enraged Finn. Finding the chip had been easy enough, but Lyra wanted to kill Claudius all over again for that alone.

Lyra wanted to force her daughter to stay close to her, to tell her to take it easy, but she was a teenager and meeting her father's pack for the first time. Vega had a right to be excited and Lyra didn't want to steal any of her daughter's joy. Plus, she didn't seem to be focusing on all the horror she'd endured. Lyra was worried it would come back to haunt Vega later, but she also knew that kids bounced back from traumatic events a hell of a lot faster than adults. "She said you gave them body-guards?"

Finn grinned at that, stepping closer, his earthy scent invading her senses as he practically circled her. Like he was a predator and she was his prey. Butterflies danced in her stomach. "Drake and Gabriel are with them so that should be interesting."

"You trust him?" She didn't need to specify she meant the unique dragon shifter.

Finn nodded, taking another step closer. Her heart drummed out of control. "I trust my gut and he seems almost reverent of all females. I know he'd die before he let anything happen to either Victoria or Vega."

"Yeah, he's insanely protective." The physical desire she felt for Finn was so strong it made her dizzy but she forced it back. She wanted him to want her because he loved her, not just because he wanted sex. "I like him." It was clear that what Drake felt for Victoria was very dif-ferent for his feelings for Vega, but Lyra could see how protective he was of her daughter. Maybe it was because they'd been in that prison cell together. Over the past couple days she'd watched with interest as he growled at anyone he thought got too close to either female. Lyra could tell it was driving Vega a little crazy, but it was fine with Lyra. She couldn't protect her daughter 24/7 and while she might have to accept that fact, it was a hell of a lot easier to live with when a powerful shifter had decided to look out for Vega.

"I'm still trying to figure out where the hell he came from and what his lineage is," Finn muttered. "And he's not much help."

Lyra wasn't surprised about that. She didn't respond; she couldn't find her voice as Finn slowly peeled his T-shirt off. The way he did it was almost like a challenge. And if he was challenging her to jump him, she had no problem with that. The moonlight illuminated the cut lines and striations of his impossibly beautiful chest and abdomen. Her mouth watered as she imagined licking and kissing a path down all that expanse of skin.

"I found out something interesting today," he said as he reached out and tugged on the tie of her robe.

How was he thinking, much less talking right now? She pushed out a long breath as he slid his finger down her chest, opening the folds of the robe. It fell open in the middle, revealing her bare mound, but still covering her breasts. Cool air hit her skin, doing nothing to bank the heat burning between them.

Finn's eyes went pure wolf as he drank her in, but he didn't make a move to do anything else. It was driving her crazy. "Turns out Vega's not the only hybrid born this century."

His words managed to penetrate her lust fogged mind. "What?"

"There's a jaguar shifter in Alabama who has—had—a vamp mother. She doesn't drink blood though and seems to be completely a shifter, but she holds a recessive vamp gene. I've asked her Alpha if we could introduce Vega to her. It might help Vega to not feel so different."

Lyra blinked at his thoughtfulness. Vega could walk in the sun and didn't have to drink as much blood as Lyra did to survive, but she still needed to imbibe it. And she had both her parents' abilities. She could turn vamp or shifter at will. It sounded as if she was different from the other hybrid, but Lyra was glad there was someone else out there her daughter could relate to. "Thank you. That's very thoughtful."

"Vega wants to start looking at colleges around here," he murmured as he reached up and pushed at the shoulders of her robe.

She shivered at the feel of his callused fingers gliding over her skin. The material pooled at her feet on the luxurious Persian rug without making a sound.

His gaze zeroed in on her breasts and his breath hitched a notch. The only sign he was affected. Well, not the only one. The visible bulge in his pants had her lower abdomen tightening with need. Why was he insisting on talking right now? She didn't want words. She wanted his face between her legs. "Okay," she rasped out.

Meeting her gaze again, he cupped one of her breasts gently and flicked his thumb over her hardening nipple. But he still kept distance between them, as if he didn't want her touching him just yet. Maybe he wanted to tease her before they got to the good stuff. That, she could handle. Even if her body was primed for him right now.

"I heard that Justus asked you to visit their coven." There was a strange note in his voice.

She nodded as her gaze fell to Finn's full lips. Her former coven member wanted to speak to her about joining in the peace treaty that so many shifter packs and vampire covens had signed a year ago. Since she'd been out of touch with the supernatural world she hadn't even known about it until Justus had told her. But she knew Finn would be more than happy to include Justus's coven now that he'd proved himself. With Claudius dead, Justus would be taking over.

Finn's eyes glowed bright blue in the dimness. "You are *not* joining his coven. You. Are. Mine." His voice turned almost guttural, hungry.

Surprised, she met his heated gaze. "I know."

"You know what?" he demanded.

Seriously, *why* did he want to talk? As he increased the pressure on her nipple she had to force herself not to press her legs together. "That I'm not joining his coven. He wanted to talk…" She shuddered when he cupped her other breast. "To talk about signing that peace treaty. I told him…" Crap, what had she told him? What were they even talking about?

Closing the distance between them, Lyra slid her hands up Finn's chest and clutched onto his shoulders. "Quit teasing me. I've been dying for a taste of you for *three* days."

His big hands moved to settle on her hips. He tugged her closer so that his erection pressed insistently between them. "So when are you moving here permanently?"

She stilled at his question. "You haven't asked me."

"I told my pack I was claiming you," he growled.

"Yeah, you told *them*, but you never discussed anything with me. Never talked about the future. It's been *three days*, Finn. I was worried you just told them that because you wanted Vega in your life. You don't have to take me as a mate to be a father to her. She clearly already loves you and I would never do anything to come between you two." Though it hurt Lyra to say the words, she wanted it clear that he had no obligation to be with her.

His jaw tightened as his fingers clenched harder into her hips. He pulled her closer and even as she cursed her weakness where he was concerned, she rubbed her breasts against his chest, needing that connection. The friction sent a spiral of hunger through her. Her fangs ached to be unleashed, to sink into his neck and bond with him. She wanted forever. Had never stopped loving the sexy, dominant, and arrogant male. But she wasn't ready to say the words yet because she wouldn't be an obligation to anyone. Her heart couldn't take it.

He leaned down until his lips brushed her ear. "You will move here, stay under my roof and protection, and we will have the family we both deserve."

Though she wanted to lean into him and kiss him senseless, she pulled back. As she looked at him she could see a stark fear she'd never witnessed from him before. He might sound arrogant, but it slammed into her that he was nervous. But she still needed to hear the words. "Why should I?"

He cleared his throat, looking suddenly tense. "I love you, Lyra. I never stopped. When I thought I lost you in that cemetery, I wanted to die with you. I want you by my side forever and I refuse to live without you. If you run from me, I'll follow."

His words rushed over her, filling her with an intense peace she'd only ever dreamed of. This is what she'd wanted to hear for so long. "Things won't be easy for us," she whispered, almost too afraid to accept the truth of his words. A female vampire as an Alpha's mate was going to cause waves no matter what they did.

"I don't want easy. I want you. And it has nothing to do with you being Vega's mother. You've always belonged to me. Time and distance didn't change that. My feelings refused to fucking die. And what I told you before was the truth about not taking other lovers. But...I did try. I thought if I could take someone else I could move on, fill that hole in my chest. I couldn't though. My wolf refused to let me even touch another female." Blunt words. True words. She could scent it coming off him in potent waves.

She rarely cried, but tears sprung up at his words. They still had a lot to discuss and she had so much to figure out, like whether she wanted to sell her bookstores or run them from a distance after she moved here. None of that mattered right now though. "I never stopped loving you, Finn. Even when I wanted to hate you, I just couldn't. Not truly. You stole part of my heart, damn you. And I don't want it back. I don't care what we have to face as long as we have each other's backs. I want to move in with you, create a family together, mate with you, and—"

Her words were lost as he crushed his mouth over hers on a low moan. Giving in to her hunger, she let her fangs descend as their tongues and bodies meshed. Arching into him, she reached between their bodies and tried to unbutton his pants. When she couldn't get the button free, she just ripped the material apart.

Finn chuckled, the deep sound spreading to all her nerve endings as he reached around her body and grabbed her ass. Hoisting her up, he moved them until they reached his massive bed.

Not quite gently, he tossed her onto it before stripping off his pants and shoes. By the time his cock sprung free she was on her knees, lunging for him. She felt consumed with the need to be filled by him. She forced her fangs back.

Grasping his hard length in her hand, she bent down and took him into her mouth. He sucked in a deep breath and slid his fingers through her hair as he cupped her head. She savored the way he shuddered each time she took him deep in her mouth. She loved that she could always get this reaction from him. That she could literally bring him to his knees.

It was the same for her. Finn completely owned her.

"Lyra," he groaned, his voice trembling.

She ignored him until he tugged on her shoulders, forcing her to look at him. The love and hunger in his eyes floored her. When she saw his canines peeking out from his lips she realized what he wanted.

To mate. Now.

Releasing her own fangs, she went with her instinct and kissed him. She knew how wolves traditionally mated, with the male taking the female from behind in a submissive gesture while the male pierced her skin with his canines. But that didn't feel right for them.

As she pressed her chest to his, sliding her fingers together behind his neck, he moved with incredible speed and repositioned them so that she was on her back and he was on top of her. She didn't have a chance to miss the feel of his body on hers.

With supernatural speed he covered her once again, his hand cupping her mound as their tongues danced together. When he slid two fingers inside her, she arched into him, loving the feel of his thick digits inside her.

But it wasn't enough. She needed everything. And she didn't want foreplay. Not with mating on the line. She wanted to be bonded to him, to be linked until one of them died. Her most primal side cried out for it.

Letting her head fall back against the soft sheets, she bared her neck to him. "Mark me, Finn. Make me yours."

Her words unleashed something inside him. Growling, he'd barely removed his fingers before he thrust inside her in one long stroke. She sucked in a deep breath as she adjusted to his size, her fingers curling around his shoulders. Her inner walls molded around him. He cupped her breasts, strumming her nipples in a way he knew drove her crazy with pleasure.

When he started slowly thrusting, she clutched onto him, pulling him closer to her. Each time he drove into her, she felt it all the way to her core, her inner walls growing slicker. His spicy scent wrapped around her, embracing her, making her lightheaded with primitive need. Feathering kisses over his chest, then shoulders, she stopped when she reached his neck. She raked her teeth over his skin, savoring the salty, earthy taste of him. Hers. He was all hers.

She was going to claim him in the same way he claimed her. Without pause she sunk her teeth into him. He shuddered in pleasure as she bit him, his body jerking against hers with no restraint. The instant his blood coated her tongue, she surged into orgasm. It took her completely off guard, the intense sensation of pleasure shooting to all her nerve endings like a shot of pure adrenaline.

"Lyra!" The way he shouted her name was so primal, she felt it all the way to her core.

As she drew his blood into her mouth, she felt his canines piercing her in the sensitive area right where her shoulder and neck met. There was no pain. Just pleasure as he sank deep in her neck, marking her for the world to see. His big body trembled against her, all those beautiful muscles rippling under the onslaught of pleasure. As quickly as she'd climaxed, he did too. His entire body jerked with the intensity of his orgasm, his thrusts wild and unsteady as he released himself inside her.

Though she hated to pull away from him, she licked the wounds she'd made, watching as they started healing, and let her head fall back. Her body was still humming, a delicious lassitude stealing through her. She cupped the back of his head. "I love you, Finn." The words didn't seem like enough to convey just how much.

He nuzzled her neck gently and let out a satisfied rumble. "Good because you're never getting rid of me."

She wasn't sure how much time passed, but eventually he pulled back and rolled off her. Instantly she missed the heavy weight of his body covering hers.

"I'll be right back," he murmured before sliding off the bed. As he turned his back to her, she frowned.

"Wait. What's on your back?" Lyra pushed up on her knees, shoving the sheets and comforter out of the way.

He stopped and turned toward her. "What is it?"

"A tattoo or something." And it hadn't been there before. She knew because she'd seen and kissed every inch of his delicious body.

At her words he went impossibly still. Then he went to a mirror on the wall. Turning, he looked at his back over his shoulder before facing her again, his expression unreadable. "Turn around," he ordered.

Unsure what he wanted, she did as he said. When she shook her butt at him, he chuckled and swatted it as he returned to the bed. She looked over her shoulder, watching him as he knelt on the edge of the mattress, his expression one of awe. He reached out and traced his finger over the middle of her back.

"What is it?" she whispered, though she wasn't sure why she was.

"You know werewolves mate for life?" When she nodded, he continued. "With true mates, destined mates, a tattoo-like symbol appears somewhere on their bodies after the first mating." His voice was thick with emotion as he spoke and she realized she had one too.

Turning, she plastered herself to him and wrapped her arms around him. "Does mine match yours?"

He nodded and gripped her tight. "Yes, it's Celtic knot work. The symbol for bonding."

Bonding. She loved the thought of being permanently linked with Finn forever in an outward display. "Is this normal for shifter mates?" When vampires mated, there wasn't an outwardly physical representation of it. The mates were just covered in their significant other's scent and other supernaturals knew they were off limits.

He shook his head. "No, it's very rare." His voice was thick with emotion, the truth of his words finally piercing through her.

They were a different species yet against all odds they'd created life together and now they had a symbol to show the world they were meant to be together, true destined mates. Not that she needed it, but she loved that it was there. It filled her with pride to know they each bore the physical mark of that bond. Things might not always be easy or perfect for them down the road, but she knew without a doubt he was perfect for her and their daughter, and that was all that mattered. "Ready to take on the world with me?"

His smile flashed in the dimness, those eyes turning pure wolf once again as he bent to whisper against her lips. "Always."

ACKNOWLEDGMENTS

Thank you so much to Kari Walker, Carolyn Crane and Joan Turner for their valuable input into this story. For my readers, thank you for reading my stories! I'm deeply grateful for your support. I'm also incredibly thankful for the beautiful design work by Jaycee with Sweet 'N Spicy Designs. She's done many of my covers and each time I wonder how she's going to top the last one. Somehow she always outdoes herself! Last, but never least, I'm thankful to God.

COMPLETE BOOKLIST

Red Stone Security Series
No One to Trust
Danger Next Door
Fatal Deception
Miami, Mistletoe & Murder
His to Protect
Breaking Her Rules
Protecting His Witness
Sinful Seduction

The Serafina: Sin City Series
First Surrender
Sensual Surrender
Sweetest Surrender

Deadly Ops Series
Targeted
Bound to Danger (2014)

Non-series Romantic Suspense
Running From the Past
Everything to Lose
Dangerous Deception

Dangerous Secrets
Killer Secrets
Deadly Obsession
Danger in Paradise
His Secret Past

Paranormal Romance
Destined Mate
Protector's Mate
A Jaguar's Kiss
Tempting the Jaguar
Enemy Mine
Heart of the Jaguar

Moon Shifter Series
Alpha Instinct
Lover's Instinct (novella)
Primal Possession
Mating Instinct
His Untamed Desire (novella)
Avenger's Heat

Darkness Series
Darkness Awakened
Taste of Darkness (2014)

ABOUT THE AUTHOR

Katie Reus is the *New York Times* and *USA Today* bestselling author of the Red Stone Security series, the Moon Shifter series and the Deadly Ops series. She fell in love with romance at a young age thanks to books she pilfered from her mom's stash. Years later she loves reading romance almost as much as she loves writing it.

However, she didn't always know she wanted to be a writer. After changing majors many times, she finally graduated summa cum laude with a degree in psychology. Not long after that she discovered a new love. Writing. She now spends her days writing dark paranormal romance and sexy romantic suspense. For more information on Katie please visit her website: www.katiereus.com. Also find her on twitter @katiereus or visit her on facebook at: www.facebook.com/katiereusauthor.

20699597R10152

Made in the USA
Middletown, DE
05 June 2015